# 151 Stories Around the World

MANOJ PUBLICATIONS

# 151 Stories Around the World

*Publisher:*

**MANOJ PUBLICATIONS**

761, Main Road, Burari, Delhi-110084
Ph.    : 91-11-27611116, 27611349
Fax    : 91-11-27611546, Mob. : 09868112194
E-mail  : info@manojpublications.com
For online shopping visit our website :
www.manojpublications.com

*Showroom :*

1583-84, Dariba Kalan, Chandni Chowk, Delhi-110006
Ph.    : 91-11-23262174, 23268216
Mob.   : 09818753569

ISBN : 978-81-310-2184-2

# CONTENTS

⓪ = not need the read the rest of the list

# 1. The Dissatisfied Devotee (Rome)

One day a woman went to the beach and began singing songs in the praise of lord Neptune. The lord was very much pleased with her. He appeared before her and asked what she wanted. The woman was happy to see the lord and asked him for a cow. The next moment there was a cow standing beside her. The woman was thrilled. She began singing another song. At the end of it there was another cow beside her. The woman went on singing and every time she stopped for breath there would be another cow on the beach. The beach was small, so it soon started getting crowded. Finally, there was just enough room for her to stand. There was a large rock at her feet. She felt that would be the place for one more cow if she removed the rock. So, she heaved it into the sea. Unfortunately, Neptune himself was coming to the surface at that moment to bestow his blessings. The rock hit him on the head. The god was so angry that he dived back into the water taking with him all the cows he had given to the woman.

## 2. The Monkeys Go Fasting (India)

One day, some monkeys decided to go on a fast. They thought that before starting the fast they should keep the food ready with which they would break the fast. So, they gathered some delicious bananas. Then they thought of sharing bananas amongst them before beginning the fast. One of them suggested that they should peel off the bananas and keep them ready to eat after the fast. So they peeled off the bananas and decided that they would not eat them under any condition before evening. A little monkey then asked if he could just keep the banana in his mouth but promised not to eat it till evening. They all liked the idea and each monkey put a banana in his mouth so that he might chew it immediately when he would break the fast. Everyone thought that as long as he did not eat it, it was fine to keep the banana in his mouth. One by one they eyed one another uncomfortably as they began their fast. As it was obvious and expected, within no time, the bananas disappeared down their gullets. This was the end of their fast.

## 3. The Wise Men of Chelm (Poland)

One day, the residents of the Jewish town of Chelm thought that there was no point in all of them separately worrying about the various problems of their lives. The mayor told that he would appoint a worry man who would be given the duty to worry for all the residents of Chelm. Everybody hailed it as a great idea. Soon the discussions began over the topic that who was the most suited person to be appointed for the duty of worrying for all. One of the elderly residents suggested that, Yossel, the cobbler should be given the job because he seemed to have a lot of time at his disposal. The mayor immediately sent his armies to fetch the cobbler. When Yossel was brought to the mayor, he was told the reason for which he was brought there. After the nature of the job was explained to him, Yossel at once asked suspiciously how much he would be paid. The mayor replied that he would pay Yossel one kopek a week. Yossel refused to do the job saying that he would have nothing to worry about if they gave him one kopek a week.

# 4. Why Cats Chase Rats (China)

Once a Chinese emperor organized a race for animals. The first twelve animals to finish were to be given a place in the Chinese Zodiac. The cat and the rat, both lazy creatures, asked the ox to wake them on the day of the race. The day arrived. The ox tried to wake them up, but could not succeed. The race was about to start. The ox coaxed them onto his back and started running. The rat woke up when the ox was crossing the last hurdle, a river. The rat pushed the cat off the ox's back. When the ox reached the other side, the rat jumped off and scampered to victory, just ahead of the ox. The tiger came third, crossing the river by using the backs of the animals swimming across as stepping stones. So the twelve-year cycle of the Chinese Zodiac begins with the rat. After him come the ox, tiger, rabbit, dragon, snake, horse, goat, monkey, rooster, dog and pig. The cat, however, has no place in the zodiac. So all the cats still remember the humiliation heaped on their ancestor by a tricky rat and thus chase the rats to punish them.

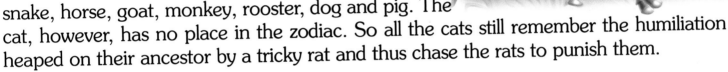

# 5. The Fisherman Who Rose too High (Europe)

Once there was an old fisherman. He would go fishing in the morning and return back in the evening. One day while fishing, he saw a large heavenly bird Kaha sitting on a rock. The bird said, "You need not do such work. From now onwards, I will bring you a big fish every evening." She began to drop a large fish at his doorstep every evening. The fisherman would take it to the market and sell it. He soon became rich. One day, he heard that the king wanted to catch Kaha bird and would reward the informer with lots of gold. The fisherman was tempted. He told the king that he could get the bird. In the evening, when the bird brought the fish, the fisherman asked her to come inside his house as he had laid out a feast for her. The moment she came to the ground, the fisherman grabbed her legs. But Kaha began flying with all strength. She rose into the air, the fisherman still clinging onto her legs. The fisherman realised that he was too high in the air to let go. Neither he nor Kaha was ever seen again.

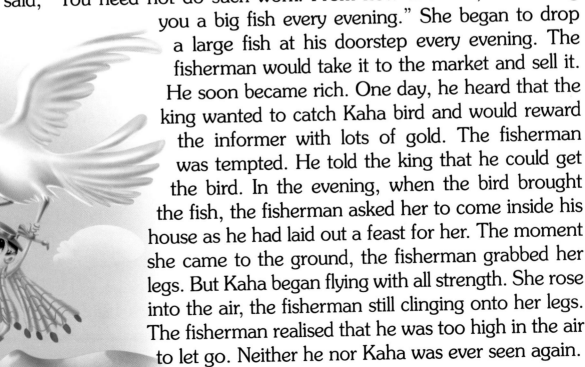

# 6. Family Misfortunes (Bhutan)

Once there lived Dough with his wife Butter, son Ant and daughter Cotton. One morning, Butter asked Ant to bring dried resin from the mepche tree. "Stay away from fresh resin to avoid getting stuck," she cautioned. Ant paid no attention. He saw a big blob of resin emerging from a crack in the tree and rushed forward to grab it. And he got stuck. When he did not return, Dough went to search for him. "Do not go near the edge of the road; you could slip and roll down the side," advised Butter. But Dough moved at the edge thinking that he was safer there. He lost his balance and went rolling down the side. When Dough also did not return, Cotton went to search for him. "Do not walk in open spaces; you could get blown away by the wind," warned Butter. Cotton did not listen and took a short cut across a meadow. A gust of wind blew her away. Butter waited for her family. The day got hotter. Butter began melting and finally turned into a puddle of liquid. This was the end of Dough family which perished because they did not follow what they were told.

# 7. Dreams (Nepal)

An owl and an elephant lived in a forest. They both were best friends. One evening, the elephant while looking for food, blundered into a gathering of demons. On seeing the elephant, the demon-king started shouting, "It's him!" "Who is he?" asked his attendants. "Last night, I dreamt I ate an elephant; it looked remarkably like this one here," said the demon. "Catch him and let me eat him so that my dream may come true." The demons caught the elephant. He was terrified. His knees began to buckle. The king, accompanied by his queen, began to advance on him. Suddenly his friend, the owl, came swooping down, shrieking, "It's her!" and settled on the elephant's head. "Who are you referring to?" the king growled. "The queen. Last night, I dreamt that I married the queen. Please allow us to marry so that my dream may come true," said the owl. "I will not marry him!" declared the queen. "And nobody is asking you to do so, dear," said the king. "Dreams are not to be taken seriously. See, here is the elephant which I ate in my dream but I am letting him go." The elephant lumbered away, muttering thanks to his friend.

# 8. The Election of the King Bird (Nigeria)

Once Essiya was the king of Calabar town. He used to call upon the animals and the birds to help his people with their work. One day, he decided to appoint head chiefs of different species. The elephant became the king of land animals and the hippopotamus became the king of water animals. But Essiya was confused about the birds. So, he called all the birds from the whole country to fight out. Many birds came, and the hawks started defeating all the birds. Soon the only birds left were the hawks and the big black-and-white fishing eagle, who was perching on a tree calmly watching everything. The hawks began swooping on one another and were badly injured. At last, they saw the fishing eagle with his terrible beak and cruel claws. Knowing his great strength, they acknowledged the fishing eagle to be their master. Essiya then declared the fishing eagle as the king bird. Thus, whenever the young men of the country go to fight, they always wear three long black-and-white feathers of the king bird in their hair, as they believe that it imparts courage to the wearer.

# 9. The Wedding of Mrs. Fox (Germany)

Once there was an old fox with nine tails, who thought that his wife was not faithful to him. In order to check, he stretched himself out under the bench and behaved as if he was dead. Mrs. Fox locked herself inside her room. Just then, someone knocked at the door. The maid, Miss Cat, opened the door and saw a young fox. He asked if Mrs. Fox was at home. The maid told that she was in her room. He then asked Miss Cat to tell Mrs. Fox that a young fox had come to marry her. She went to Mrs. Fox and conveyed the message. Mrs. Fox asked if he had nine tails. "No, he has only one," answered the cat. Mrs. Fox rejected him. The maid sent the young fox away. After this, more animals came, each with one tail more than the last one, until a fox came with nine tails. When the widow heard that, she joyfully asked the cat to prepare the wedding feast. But just as the wedding was going to be solemnized, old Mr. Fox stirred under the bench, and drove away all the guests and Mrs. Fox out of the house.

# 10. Wish List (France)

Once after winning a great battle, Napoleon Bonaparte was in a generous mood. He asked his four officers to ask for anything and he promised to give it. His German officer asked for a bungalow in Paris. The French officer asked to own a hotel. His Pole officer asked for a brewery "Done!" said the emperor, "I will fulfil your desires!" Then he asked the desire of his fourth officer who was a Jew. He asked for a fortnight's leave. The emperor told that his leave began from the next day. His colleagues were surprised. They asked him why he had asked for so little. The Jew replied that the emperor was a busy man. He would order his secretary who was a busy man too to fulfil the promises. He would pass on the order to his assistant who too was a busy man. So the emperor's order would go down from one subordinate to the other and by then, the great victory would have become a dim memory. So, he asked for something that the emperor could give immediately. Then leaving the three officers gaping, the Jew went off to arrange for his holiday.

# 11. The Sun-Goddess of Korea (Korea)

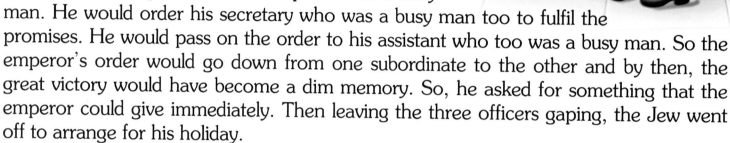

Byun Soon, Dael Soon and Hae Soon were three sisters. One day, a tiger came to their house. The girls were frightened to see the tiger. They ran out of the back door and climbed up a tree. When the tiger began to climb up the tree, the sisters prayed to the god to save them. Their prayers were answered. An iron chain descended from the skies and the sisters climbed up to safety. They lived happily in the land of the gods. In due time, Byun Soon was transformed into a star, Dael Soon into the moon and Hae Soon into the sun. When Hae Soon set out across the skies on her first day out as the sun, people on earth came out of their homes to stare at her. Hae Soon was an extremely shy girl and she turned pale with embarrassment when she saw the people looking up at her. The more they stared, the brighter she became, till she became so bright that the people were blinded by her radiance and could no longer look up. This suited the shy Hae Soon and she continued to glow brightly from then on.

# 12. Double Trouble (Indonesia)

Once there lived a man named Jamal with his wife Fatima. One day, Fatima asked her husband to dig the patch of land outside their hut to plant some vegetables. Jamal agreed. He took a spade and started digging. The spade suddenly struck a metal. Jamal excitedly scraped away the mud and saw a big cooking pot. As Jamal leaned over, his pouch of tobacco fell into it. Jamal bent to retrieve it and was surprised to see two pouches. "Come quickly!" he called to Fatima, "Look what I have found!" Fatima was excited. She put some coins in four or five times. Soon there was a tidy pile of money. She stooped to collect the coins, lost her balance and fell inside the pot. Soon there were two Fatimas, a complete mirror image of each other.

Jamal stood confused for a moment and then jumped into the pot. Soon there were two Jamals. The new Jamal and his wife asked for an identical set of possessions. But how did he recognise his wife? As she was a mirror image, her nose ring was on the left nostril. But the real Fatima had always worn it on the right.

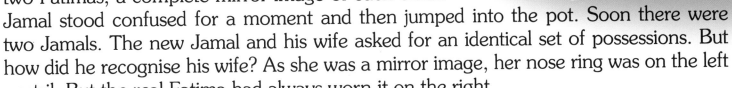

# 13. Learning from the Enemy (Japan)

Once a samurai warrior killed his master. He knew that he would be put to death if he was caught. So he fled and reached a remote village that was separated from the rest of the world by a mountain. The path across the mountain was narrow and treacherous. The warrior decided to cut a road single-handedly through the mountain. He worked hard for four years and penetrated halfway into the mountain. One morning, his master's son came to him to take revenge. The samurai said that he surely deserved death but asked his master's son to wait until he had completed the tunnel. The son agreed. He watched the samurai with his hard work and began to develop a respect for him. He started helping the samurai. Years passed and they finally broke through to the other side. The isolation of the remote village had finally ended. The samurai was ready to die now. He asked his enemy to kill him. The Master's son said that the samurai was his enemy earlier but now he had learnt much from him in the last few years. So, he could not kill his teacher and went away.

# 14. Advice (Italy)

Once there was a great battle amongst animals. After the war had ended, a porcupine and a fox were returning back together from the battlefield to their respective dwelling places. The fox had an evil thought of killing the porcupine. But the fox was worried about the coat of sharp spines on the porcupine's body that would not only protect the porcupine but also injure the fox. However, the fox was very clever. The fox thought for a while and devised a trick. Pointing at the coat of spines, the cunning fox asked the porcupine why he was wearing that armour of spines. The porcupine told that it protected him against the deadly wars of cunning creatures. The fox flattered the porcupine by saying that the war was over and harmony established in the forest. So, he should remove the heavy armour and feel relaxed. The innocent porcupine was unfortunately convinced by the fox's advice and took off his armour. The fox promptly pounced on him and killed him in no time. Therefore, it is said to beware of advice from those who have their own interest at heart.

# 15. Totally Useful Youth (Malaysia)

Once there was a kind youth. He was always keen on helping others. One day, he was strolling near a lonely hut. He saw an old man in front of the hut. The youth thought that the old man must be some learned sage. He asked the old man, "Sir, I want to be good to all. How can I do that?" The old man went inside his hut. He came out with an elegant casket, which was latched. He handed it over to the youth and said, "Take this casket home carefully and open it. Then, you will know what to do. But remember not to open it on the way." The youth thanked the old man and carried the casket away. But, on the way, he wondered what could be there inside. He could not suppress his curiosity. He opened it, completely forgotten about the warning of the old man. As soon as the casket was opened, the youth was transformed into a strange tall plant. He became a coconut tree with leaves and nuts at an unreachable height. Today, we all are very well familiar with this most useful tree.

# 16. Why Crows are Black (Myanmar)

Once, Sun fell in love with a princess. The princess too became quite fond of him. The Sun decided to send her a blood-red Ruby stone as a token of his love for her. He put the gem in a silken bag and asked a crow to deliver it to his beloved. In those days, a crow had milky white feathers and it was considered a sacred bird. As the crow began flying, he smelled delicious food from a wedding feast. It kept the bag on a tree and went to eat the food. A merchant saw the bag and was overjoyed to see its contents. He took out the ruby, filled the bag with dry cow dung and put the bag on the tree. When the crow returned, he took the bag and reached the princess. She took the bag eagerly. But when she saw its contents, she reeled back in anger. She flung

the bag away, rushed to her palace, and never came out again. When the Sun learnt of the incident, he was furious and turned his scorching gaze on the crow resulting in his feathers burnt black. So the crow's feathers have been black ever since.

# 17. Disputed Waters (Persia)

One day, a clever man sold a well to a farmer. The farmer was pleased that now he could get plenty of water for his crops. He went to the well to draw out some water. But the man, who had sold him the well, stopped him and said that he had sold him the well but not its water. So, if he wanted to draw out water, he would have to pay separately for that. The farmer, of course, refused to pay extra for the water. They quarrelled over the matter for a long time but no conclusion could be drawn out. So, the case was taken to a Qazi. After hearing both sides the Qazi realised the cleverness of the man who had sold the well to the poor farmer. So, he said to the man that since he had sold only the well, he had no right to keep his water in it. He asked the man to pay rent to the farmer for using his well or to take his water out at once. The man realised that he had been outwitted. He bowed to the Qazi and quietly left the court.

# 18. Making Haste Slowly (Philippines)

Once a trader bought a large number of coconuts. He loaded them onto his horse cart and set off for his home in the village. A little later, he encountered a small boy on the road. He asked the boy how long it would take to reach the main road. "Go slowly and you will reach the main road in ten minutes," replied the boy, "but if you go fast, it will take you half an hour or more." The trader thought that the boy was surely a fool. So, he decided to double up his pace and drove away at a great speed. Suddenly, fifty metres down the road, one of the wheels of his cart struck a stone. The coconuts could not bear the sudden accidental jolt and the next moment the trader saw his coconuts lying in all directions. It took him a very long time to gather all the coconuts and put them back in the cart. He was very much tired after the whole process. He climbed back wearily into the driver's seat, and with the boy's words ringing in his ears, drove slowly and cautiously the rest of the way.

# 19. Why do Kangaroos Hop? (Australia)

One day, a baby kangaroo named Kip asked his mother why kangaroos hop. "We are kangaroos," his mother replied simply, "That is what we do." Kip went to his friend Kimmy Koala and asked if he could hop. Kimmy replied that he could neither hop nor run. He could just climb up trees. Kip then saw Cedric Crocodile and asked whether he could hop. Cedric replied that he could only swim and crawl but he could not run or hop. Next, Kip asked Danny Dingo if he could hop. Danny replied that he could run and walk but could not hop. Kip then went to Kara Kookaburra and asked if he could hop. The bird replied that he could only fly but not hop. Kip happily thought that none of his friends could hop. Only kangaroos had the ability. He felt very special. He hopped all the way home. "Dingos, crocodiles, koalas and kookaburras cannot hop. I am happy that I am a kangaroo and can hop all over the place," Kip told his mother. His mother smiled at him. Kip spent the rest of the day hopping about the bush, enjoying being a simple kangaroo.

# 20. Passport (Russia)

One day, a dim-witted wolf saw a horse grazing in a field. His mouth watered as he thought of eating him. When the horse saw the wolf approaching him, he sensed that the wolf intended to eat him. The horse at once used his wits and thought of a plan. When the wolf tried to attack the horse, he said to the wolf, "You cannot eat me." "But why?" asked the wolf. The horse confidently replied that he had a passport. "What is a passport?" asked the wolf. The horse said that he would show him his passport if you came and stood behind me. The wolf was curious to know what a passport was. So, he followed the horse's instruction and stood behind him. He saw the long hairy tail of the horse and wondered if perhaps the horse's tail was the passport. Suddenly, the horse kicked him hard on his face. The wolf screamed out loudly as his two teeth shot out of his mouth. He laid on the grass crying in pain while the horse ran away as fast as he could and finally vanished from the sight of the injured wolf.

# 21. Tug of War (West Africa)

Once there was a rabbit who enjoyed playing tricks on others. One day, he went to an elephant and said, "You are certainly a powerful animal but not more powerful than I. The elephant began to laugh. The rabbit said, "I will tie a rope around your middle and drag you into the sea." "Well, go ahead!," the elephant allowed. He tied a rope around the elephant's body and ran to the seashore with the other end of the rope. He saw a whale and called it out, "Hey! Can you prove yourself stronger than I?" said the rabbit, "I will tie this rope around your middle and drag you ashore." The whale began laughing. "All right; go ahead," he allowed. The rabbit tied the rope securely and hid behind a tree and shouted, "PULL!" The elephant wrapped his trunk around the rope and gave a mighty heave upwards. The whale countered with a tug that almost brought the elephant to his knees. The two animals were amazed at the rabbit's strength. They exerted their strength to the utmost and the rope broke. The two animals fled in opposite directions. The rabbit was greatly amused.

# 22. Wild Edric (England)

Wild Edric was a famous champion. One day, he lost his way in the forest and wandered alone. He saw a large house and reached there. There, he saw some beautiful ladies dancing. He fell in love with one of the most beautiful of them. He snatched the maiden from her place and escaped with his captive. The maiden said to Edric, "You will be lucky as long as I am with you but if you reproach me on account of my sisters, you will lose both your bride and your good fortune and will pine away quickly to an early death." He promised never to do so and solemnly wedded in the presence of all the nobles from far and wide, invited to their bridal feast. One evening, Edric returned from hunting, and could not find his wife. He called her for some time and she finally arrived. Edric said angrily, "Did your sisters detain you for such a long time?" The moment her sisters were mentioned, his wife vanished. Edric's grief was overwhelming. He cried out and pined away, and soon died of sorrow.

# 23. The Beggar and the Miser (Arabia)

Once there was an utterly poor and old beggar. One day, he passed through an old village. He knocked at the door of a big beautiful house, with a tall barn and a large iron padlock on the gate. In this house lived a man, who was famous in the village for his miserliness and never helped people, even though he was very rich. "Please give me some meat or milk," said the beggar. The miser replied roughly, "No, I cannot! Go away!" "Maybe you can give me some wheat or beans," kept asking the beggar, forced by hunger to humiliate himself. "I do not have anything to give you," said the miser. "Then give me a loaf of bread, and I will be highly grateful," said the beggar. "Go away; I do not have any bread at home," was the miser's reply. "At least give me some water. I am very thirsty," "I do not have water," screamed the miser. Then said the beggar, "Oh, my son, why are you sitting here then? Stand up and start begging food from the good people. You are even poorer than I am."

# 24. The Rabbit and the Moon (Canada)

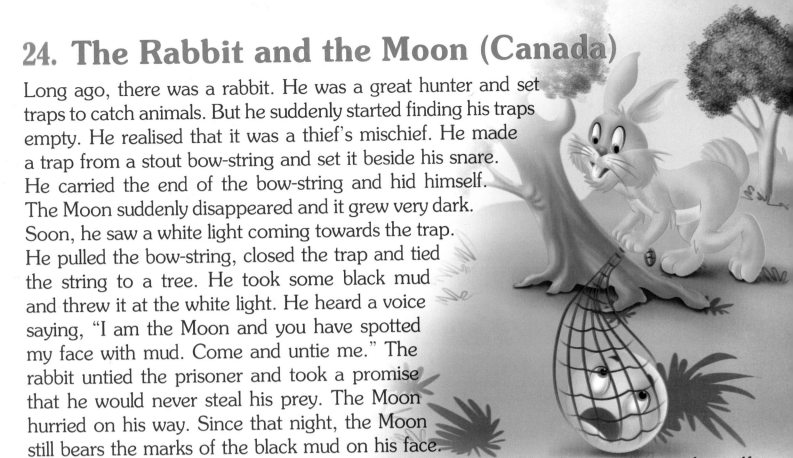

Long ago, there was a rabbit. He was a great hunter and set traps to catch animals. But he suddenly started finding his traps empty. He realised that it was a thief's mischief. He made a trap from a stout bow-string and set it beside his snare. He carried the end of the bow-string and hid himself. The Moon suddenly disappeared and it grew very dark. Soon, he saw a white light coming towards the trap. He pulled the bow-string, closed the trap and tied the string to a tree. He took some black mud and threw it at the white light. He heard a voice saying, "I am the Moon and you have spotted my face with mud. Come and untie me." The rabbit untied the prisoner and took a promise that he would never steal his prey. The Moon hurried on his way. Since that night, the Moon still bears the marks of the black mud on his face. Sometimes, he goes away to wash off the mud. But he never succeeds in cleaning himself and when he comes back to his work, the black marks are still upon his shining face.

# 25. The Boy and the Violin (Brazil)

Once there was a poor boy. He owned nothing but a violin. One day, the boy went to a forest and began playing his violin. The flock of sheep, that were grazing at some distance, heard the music and started dancing to the tune. They followed the sound and reached the boy. He continued to play the melodious music. Soon other beasts of the forest began dancing to the tune and joined the gay procession. The jolly procession wandered on and finally reached the king of the land of the giants. The king was amused and laughed hard at the sight. The king had a daughter who remained sad all the time. All the giants had done their very funniest tricks but could not make her smile. So, the king took the little boy to her sad daughter. When she saw the sight, a happy smile played about her lips. The king was happy to see her daughter and gave half of his kingdom to the boy. The boy, from that time on, reigned over half of the kingdom. He played on his violin to his people. All the beasts stayed in his kingdom forever.

# 26. The Three Snake Leaves (Germany)

Once there was a princess. She wished to marry a man who could bury himself alive with her if she died first. A youth promised to fulfil her desire and they were soon married. Some years later, the princess died. Her husband was buried alive with her. Inside the grave, a snake crept and the youth killed it. Then another snake arrived carrying three green leaves. It put the leaves on the mouth of the dead snake who became alive again. Both the snakes hastened away together. The youth picked up the leaves and laid them on the mouth of his dead wife and she became alive.

They both were taken out of the grave carrying the three snake leaves. But the princess was now changed. She no longer loved her husband. She conspired and killed him. But a servant saw her and with the help of the three snake-leaves, he brought the youth back to life. The two then went to the princess. She was thunderstruck. The youth put her in a ship which had been pierced with holes. The ship was sent out to the sea, where it soon sank amid the waves.

# 27. The Serpent (Italy)

Once there was a serpent who fell in love with a princess. He went to the king and expressed his love for the princess and his desire to marry her. The king put up conditions that seemed impossible for him to be fulfilled. But the serpent fulfilled them all. So, the king had to agree for the marriage. Soon after this, the serpent shook off his skin and turned into a handsome prince. The king burnt the serpent's skin. Seeing this, the prince turned into a dove and flew out of the window where he struck his head through the panes and injured him. The princess set out to find her love. She took the blood of forest birds, went to the royal palace and entered the chamber of the prince where he was lying unconscious. She applied the blood on his wound. Soon the wound healed without even leaving a mark. The prince regained his senses. He saw the beautiful princess and recognised his beloved at once. He embraced her with joy. Then the prince's father sent to invite the princess's parents and they celebrated their wedding with wonderful festivity.

# 28. The Toy-Goose (Denmark)

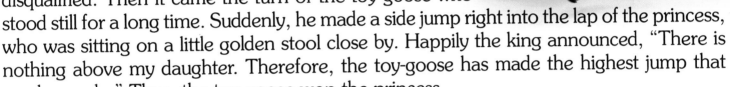

Once a flea, a grasshopper and a toy-goose got into an argument. They wanted to see which one of them could jump the highest. So, they decided to have a competition and invited the whole world to see the frolic. "Well, I will give my daughter to the one who jumps the highest," said the king, "For it would not be fair to let these people jump for nothing." The trial was to take place. The flea was given the first opportunity and he jumped. But unfortunately, he jumped so high that none could see where he went to. So, they said that he had not jumped at all. After that, the grasshopper jumped half as high and landed on the king's face which angered the king and he was disqualified. Then it came the turn of the toy-goose who stood still for a long time. Suddenly, he made a side jump right into the lap of the princess, who was sitting on a little golden stool close by. Happily the king announced, "There is nothing above my daughter. Therefore, the toy-goose has made the highest jump that can be made." Thus, the toy-goose won the princess.

# 29. The Wise King of Leon (Spain)

Once a king's barber fell in love with a princess who was equally fond of him. But the king did not like it. So, the couple left the palace and went to the forest. On their way, the couple exchanged their clothes and went to the king of Leon. The princess offered her services to the king as barber. The king willingly accepted the services. The barber, however, told that he was the princess of Castille. The King of Leon fell in love with her and told this to the barber. When everyone in the palace had slept, they again exchanged their clothes and came back in their real forms. The king got up earlier than usual. The princess presented herself before the king. On seeing her, the king asked who she was and where the barber was. At this moment the real barber presented himself. Then they both stepped forward and explained everything to the king. The king said, "I have been shaved by the King of Castille's daughter, and I have loved his barber. I will not be again deceived. They shall now be husband and wife for ever." This was the wise King of Leon.

# 30. The Magician and the Sultan's Son (Tanzania)

Once there was a sultan who had three little sons. One day a magician offered to teach reading and writing to his sons. He asked for one of his sons as his fees. The sultan agreed. In a short time, the magician turned them into great scholars. The sultan took his two sons that he preferred, and the magician took the third to his own house and named him Keejaanaa. The magician gave all the keys to Keejaanaa as he had to go away for a month. When he was gone, Keejaanaa took the keys and went to examine the house. The first room he opened contained liquid gold. One room had a horse who told Keejaanaa that the magician was a man and beast eater. This scared Keejaanaa. They made a plan. When the magician arrived, they suddenly pushed him in a pot of boiling butter and killed him. The horse swallowed all the liquid gold and they both ran away. The horse coughed up all the gold he had swallowed, with which they purchased slaves and cattle, and everything they needed. They lived very happily together and Keejaanaa loved the horse as his own soul.

# 31. The President Who Had Horns (Philippines)

Once there was a president who was very unjust to his people. One day, he angrily said that he wished to have horns so that he might frighten his people. Soon, his wish was granted and two sharp horns began to grow on his head. While trimming the president's hair, his barber discovered this but the president threatened him that he would be killed if he told anyone about the horns. The barber did not intend to tell anyone but he could not resist himself. So, he went to the field and dug a hole under some bamboo. He then crawled in and whispered that the president had horns. He then climbed out, filled up the hole, and went home. But now anyone who passed the bamboo stopped there, hearing a voice from the trees that said president had horns. Soon, the news spread all over the town. The councilmen went to see the president because then the president had no right to govern the people if the rumour of the horns was true. When they saw the horns on the president's head, they killed him as he was no better than an animal.

# 32. The Mermaid Wife (Scotland)

One day, a man saw some mermen and mermaids dancing and several seal-skins strewed beside them on the ground. At his approach, they took their seal-skins and plunged into the sea. But one skin still lay there which he carried with him. On returning to the shore he met a beautiful maiden. She was the mermaid who was exiled as she had lost her seal-skin. The man fell in love with her beauty and asked her to marry him. Perceiving that she must become an inhabitant of the earth, she accepted his proposal and they soon married. The couple had several children. But the mermaid would often go secretly to meet a large seal in the sea and talk with him. One day, their sons found a seal-skin hidden in their house and took it to his mother. She burst forth into an ecstasy of joy. She hastily embraced her children and fled towards the sea. The husband ran to overtake her but she told him that she loved him a lot but she always loved her first seal husband more. She then dived to unknown depths with her seal husband.

# 33. The Necklace of Pearls (Portugal)

Once there lived a woman with her son Francisco. He was a handsome boy. He went fishing daily. Once he went fishing at night. After being tired, he slept in his boat. A water-nymph saw the handsome youth and was attracted towards him. She gently drew him to her palace. Francisco's mother was grief-stricken. She went to the Wiseman of the Sea and asked for help. He told her that Francisco was given a philtre by a water-nymph which had made him forget his past life. He suggested that the lady should shed her tears in the sea that might fall upon Francisco's heart and he would regain his past memory. The woman shed tears and soon Francisco was safe at home. Some years later, he fell in love with a rich man's daughter who wanted a husband for her daughter that could bring her a precious gift. So, Francisco was upset. The water-nymph realised the cause of his grief. Next morning Francisco saw a necklace of priceless pearls on the shore. It was the gift of the water-nymph. He took the gift to the rich man and married his daughter.

## 34. The Lady Farmer (Wales)

Kaddy was a lady farmer. One day, she went to the forest to gather sticks for her fire. While she was gathering the sticks, she found a piece of gold and was overjoyed. She took it home but she never told anyone that she had found a gold piece for she always pretended to be very poor. Though she was so poor yet she used to dress two of her children in fine clothes, but the others whom she did not like, she kept in the filthiest rags. One day, a man knocked at her door and asked to see her children. He sat down in her little room and she went and brought the ragged little boy and girl saying that she was very poor and could not afford to dress them better. She was very cautious and carefully hid her two well-dressed little boy and girl in a cockloft. After the stranger had gone, she went to the cockloft to look for her well-dressed favourite kids but they had disappeared from there. Kaddy repented her action of lying to the stranger but it was too late for her to realise her mistake.

## 35. The Cat and the Cradle (Netherlands)

Once in Friesland, a baby-girl was born in a family. The couple was glad but the grandmother was angry and wished to kill her. So, the parents gave the baby to a woman who took her to her home. The father secretly made her a cradle. The parents came often to see her. There was a cat in the house. She was very fond of the baby-girl. One day, a great flood came when the baby-girl was sound asleep. The cat leaped upon her cradle and they floated off together. They swept into a place in front of a church and the cat began to meow. In the church, a small boy named Dirck heard the sound and rushed to pick the cradle and the cat up. He took them to her mother. The baby was welcomed in the family. She grew up to be a beautiful woman and was married to Dirck. When their son was born, he laid in her mother's cradle. The cat looked after the baby-boy just as she had looked after her mother. When the cat died, her statue was chiselled in the church which stands there even today.

# 36. The Husband Who was to Mind the House (Norway)

Once a man and his wife exchanged their work. The wife went out with the mowers and the man began churning the butter. He felt thirsty, so he turned on the tap. A pig came into the kitchen and knocked the churn over. He began churning again. But he had to draw water from the well. He took the churn on his back and went to draw out water but the cream ran over his shoulders and into the well. He took his cow to feed on the grass on the thatched roof. He put the water to boil to make porridge and then went to the cow. He tied one end of the rope to the cow's neck and the other he slipped down the chimney and tied round his own thigh. He began to grind the oatmeal. But the cow fell off the house-top and dragged the man up the chimney by the rope. When the wife arrived home, she saw the cow hanging, ran up and cut the rope. Due to this, her husband came down the chimney. When she came inside the kitchen, her husband was standing with his head in the porridge pot.

# 37. The Toad and Diamonds (France)

Once there was a widow who had two daughters. The eldest resembled her mother as both were disagreeable and proud. The youngest resembled her father as both were courteous, sweet and beautiful. Mother loved her elder daughter and disliked the younger. She made her work hard a lot. One day, the younger daughter gave water to a poor thirsty woman who was a fairy in disguise. Pleased with her, she told that a diamond would come out of her mouth at every word she would speak. Now the fairy's words came true and the girl told the whole story to her mother. The mother sent her elder daughter too to help the poor woman. But the fairy appeared to her in the form of a princess and discovered that she was rude and not service-minded. She told that a toad would come out of her mouth at every word she would speak. When the mother heard this, she beat her younger daughter. She left home and went to hide herself in the forest. There, she met a prince and told him her whole story. The prince took her to his palace and married her.

# 38. The Twelve Months (Czech Republic)

Once there was a lady who had an ugly daughter named Holena. She also had a beautiful step-daughter named Marushka. The lady and Holena behaved in evil manner with Marushka. Once during January, Holena sent Marushka to bring her violets. Marushka wandered in the cold and saw twelve men sitting. They were the Twelve Months. Marushka went to them and told her problem. March waved a staff and soon violets began to grow. Holena was amazed when Marushka brought the violets. She sent her again to bring strawberries. Marushka brought them with June's help. Holena sent her to bring apples. She brought them with September's help. Seeing this, Holena herself went out and met the twelve months. But she behaved rudely with them. Thus, angered, January waved a staff and an icy wind blew and snow began to fall. Holena could not reach her cottage. Her mother too came out to find Holena. At home, Marushka prayed for her sister and mother but they did not come. They both were frozen to death on the mountain. After some years, Marushka married a farmer. He proved to be a good husband and they lived together very happily.

# 39. The Disobedient Rooster (Slovakia)

Once there were a rooster and a hen who were very good friends. They were more like brother and sister. The rooster was careless and often did foolish things while the hen was sincere and always advised the rooster not to do so. One day, they went to a garden and saw green gooseberries. The hen instructed the rooster not to eat the green gooseberries as they could pain his stomach. But the rooster kept on eating the gooseberries and at last got a terrible pain in his stomach. The hen gave him medicine and the rooster was healthy again. One day, they went out to the meadow and the rooster ran until he got all overheated. He went to drink cold water but the hen instructed him not to drink cold water when he was overheated. But the rooster did not listen. He got a chill and it took a long time to become healthy again. One day, he went to slide on ice and the hen asked him to wait till the ice got harder. But he did not listen. Unfortunately, the ice broke and the rooster fell into the river and was drowned.

# 40. The Girl and the Snake (Sweden)

Once there was a girl who went in the forest and lost her way. She arrived at a hill and saw a door and went in. There was a table covered with tasty food. There was a bed in which lay a great snake. The snake said to the girl, "Sit down, if you choose. Eat, if you choose. Lie down in the bed, if you choose. But if you do not choose, then do not do so." So the girl did nothing at all. The snake then said, "Some people are coming who want to dance with you. But do not go along with them." Straightway people arrived who wanted to dance with the girl but she did not agree. She left the hill and went home. The following day, she again went  to the forest and arrived at the same hill. But this time, she ate the food and lay on the bed. The girl gave a loving touch to the snake who soon turned into a handsome youth. He was a prince, bewitched in the form of a snake by magic spells. Then both of them went away and there was nothing further heard of them.

# 41. The Magic Mirror (Spain)

Once there was a king of Granada. He decided to get married. The news spread throughout the kingdom. The king had a magic mirror into which if any woman, not being thoroughly good, would look, the blemishes on her character would appear in the form of many spots on its surface. So, it was decided that each woman of the kingdom, who was willing to become the king's wife, would gaze into the mirror. Although the king was a very handsome man yet no woman applied to have a look into the mirror, fearing that it may highlight her character traits. The king was very upset. One day, his barber suggested that there 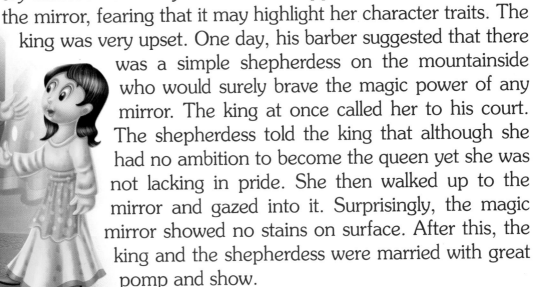 was a simple shepherdess on the mountainside who would surely brave the magic power of any mirror. The king at once called her to his court. The shepherdess told the king that although she had no ambition to become the queen yet she was not lacking in pride. She then walked up to the mirror and gazed into it. Surprisingly, the magic mirror showed no stains on surface. After this, the king and the shepherdess were married with great pomp and show.

# 42. The Hair Transplant (India)

Once a weaver was busy making a blanket. A saint came and told the weaver that he wanted to stay there in order to see how he made a blanket. The weaver allowed and turned back to his work. The saint, secretly, pulled out several tufts of his long hair and mixed them with the wool weaver was using. The weaver then took the blanket to the market to sell. The saint followed him and told that he wanted to see how he sold a blanket. An elderly man, after haggling interminably over the price, agreed to buy it. "Now please give me my share," said the saint to the weaver. "What share?" asked the weaver. "Have you not used some of my hair to make the blanket?" Saying so, the saint snatched the blanket from the buyer and showed the hair that had been woven into it. The weaver was so angry that he felt like pulling out the rest of the saint's hair. But he controlled himself and not wishing to make a scene in front of the customer, gave a few rupees in the saint's hand and sent him away.

# 43. Why Dogs Sniff (Portugal)

Once upon a time, the dogs arranged a party. Everything had been arranged with the utmost care. All the good things to eat were spread. The sun was shining brightly and a soft gentle little breeze was blowing. There was a cross fussy old dog who came to the

party. Nothing ever suited him. Whenever he went to a party, he always found fault with something. There was always something wrong for him. At this party, however, everything seemed to be exactly as it should be. But he noticed immediately that the big juicy bone he was eating had not been seasoned with pepper. "Will somebody please pass the pepper?" he asked. All the dogs tried to find the pepper but there was no pepper at that party. So one dog decided to go into the city to get some pepper. None ever knew which dog it was. The dog never returned to the party again. Since then, whenever two dogs meet they always sniff at each other hoping that if one of them happens to be the dog who went to get the pepper, he would surely carry the smell of pepper.

# 44. The Sleeping Knights (Poland)

Once a stranger went to a blacksmith and gave him a gold bar to make a horseshoe from it. He promised to pay a great amount but the blacksmith must promise not to tell anyone. The blacksmith agreed. When the horseshoe was made, the stranger took him to a cave. Inside, an army of knights were sleeping, holding battle axes and spears. There were beautiful sleeping horses with their horseshoes made of gold. The stranger asked the blacksmith to replace the broken shoe of one horse. The stranger told him that the knights had been in a deep sleep for hundreds of years and they would wake when time came for a great battle. The knights would then come out of the cave to fight for Poland. The stranger then took the blacksmith back to his village and made him swear never to tell anyone what he had seen. He gave the blacksmith a bag of gold and vanished. The blacksmith, however, could not keep the secret. So, his bag of gold soon turned to sand and he searched for the cave many times but never able to find it.

# 45. The Teacher and the Student (China)

In a school, there was a teacher who loved to have a snack and a nap afterwards. Every time, before the lessons, he ate and after the beginning of the lessons, he slept until the bell for the end of the lessons sounded. One day, a student named Lee asked the teacher why he slept during the lessons. The teacher replied that during these minutes he met the Buddha and listened to his wise words; that is why he tried to sleep as much as he could. One day, Lee took care of his sick father during the night and fell asleep at school in the morning. He slept so deeply that he did not hear the bell, which woke the teacher up. When the teacher saw the sleeping boy, he got very angry, took Lee by the ear and started screaming, "Ah, you, little weasel! How dare you fall asleep in my class?" Lee said, "It just seemed that I slept. I was with the Buddha and listened to his wise words." "What did the Almighty Buddha say to you?" asked the teacher. "He told me never in my life have I seen your teacher," Lee replied.

# 46. Not True (Japan)

Mr. Kitchom loved to listen to stories, but at the end of each tale, he always exclaimed, "That cannot be true." One day, he asked his teacher to tell him a story. He agreed on a condition that Mr. Kitchom should not say 'That cannot be true' at the end otherwise he would have to pay a penalty. Mr. Kitchom agreed. The story began: "One day, an aristocrat was going to the governor's palace in his palanquin. On the way, he heard a bird crying. When he peered out, the bird soiled his robe with its droppings. He sent his servant for a new robe and put it on. A little later, the bird cried again and when he peered out, it soiled his sword with its droppings. He sent his servant back for another sword. After sometime, the bird came out again and dropped its load on his head. He sent his servant to bring a new head and cut off his own." "That cannot be true," exclaimed Mr. Kitchom. The teacher said triumphantly, "You have uttered the prohibited phrase and you agreed to pay some penalty." Mr. Kitchom said slyly, "Oh! That cannot be true."

# 47. The Tiger's Whiskers (Korea)

There was an old hermit in Korea. One day, a woman pleaded with the hermit to help her regain her husband's affection. The hermit said that he could make a potion that could kindle love in the person who consume it but he lacked a tiger's whisker that was one of the ingredients to go into its making. The woman promised to get the whisker. She saw a tiger near the river and was frightened. She brought him food and soon they had become good friends. She patted his head and ran her hand down the side of his face. One day, she deftly pulled out one of his whiskers. She rushed to the hermit's house and gave him the whisker. He dropped it into fire. "What have you done!" said the woman, "You promised to make me a magic potion!" The hermit said softly that she did not need any potion. Because through her gentleness and patience she could win her husband's affection who surely was more responsive than a savage and blood-thirsty tiger. The woman returned home. When she saw her husband, she remembered the tiger and the hermit's words and moved forward with a smile on her face.

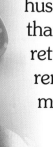

# 48. Immune to Flattery (Myanmar)

A king was told that a man who had made a career of flattery was coming to his palace. "Be on your guard," warned his advisers, "This fellow wins the favour of everyone through his flattery and then gets them to part with costly gifts." "I am too hard-headed to fall for such tricks," said the king, "Let him come." When the man came, he fell at the king's feet. "How honoured I am to be in the same room as the mightiest of monarchs," he intoned, "I find myself blinded by the radiance of your beauty, the glory of your presence, your divine charm, your grace, your elegance." He went on in this fashion for about

twenty minutes. When he paused for breath, one of the advisers seized the opportunity to have a quick word with his royal master. "Didn't we warn you, Your Majesty," he said, "He is a glib talker." "Have no fear," replied the king, "As I told you, it's not easy to trick me. The moment he starts to flatter me, I will throw him out. But so far he has spoken nothing but the truth."

# 49. Top Questions (Nepal)

Once Bhupendra Prasad asked his daughter-in-law, "Can you guess how much I spent on your wedding?" "About the cost of a sack of rice," she replied. He thought she was a nitwit. He asked her to explain it. "What you spent on the essentials of the marriage amounted to a few hundred rupees only," answered the woman, "The rest you spent to enhance your prestige that was not on the marriage but on yourself." A few weeks later, they all met up with a funeral procession when the daughter-in-law asked a mourner, "Is it just one corpse or a hundred?" Bhupendra was greatly embarrassed and asked the reason for her folly. She told, "Some people have many dependents. When they die, their dependents also die." Then they came upon labourers working in a field. "Are you reaping this year's harvest or last year's?" asked the daughter-in-law. He was angry. But she explained, "These labourers are perennially in debt. I was enquiring whether they were working to pay off the last year's debt or had paid it all and were beginning anew." Bhupendra was highly impressed by her intelligence and wisdom.

29

# 50. The Lost Message (South Africa)

The ant has always had many enemies like birds, anteaters, centipedes, hunting-spiders, lizards and many more. Frightened with all of them, all the ants of the world once held a meeting or conference to find out the place of safety. But they could come to no decision because the discussion was a true babel of diversity and each variety of ant had its own different suggestion. So, each party resolved to go to work in its own way. They chose a king in each party and divided the labour so that all the work might go smoothly but they forgot to think of protecting themselves against the onslaught of enemies. The red-ants lived under the ground but the anteaters approached them. The wagtail-ants fled to the trees, but the centipedes and the birds easily found them. The grey-ants took to flight, but the lizard, the hunting-spider, and the birds could fly faster than they. At last, the insect-king sent them the message of unity through a beetle. But unfortunately, he never arrived at the the place of ants. So, the ants are still the prey of their enemies.

# 51. The Tree with the Agate Beads (Philippines)

One day a man with his faithful dog went to the mountains to hunt. He saw a deer. He threw his spear and pierced the deer's body but he did not fall. Instead, he ran and plunged into a hole in the ground. The man and his dog followed. They entered into a large spacious room. He found a small tree on which berries grew. Astonished at finding anything growing below the ground, he broke off a branch and as he did so the shrub began to talk to him. Terrified, the man ran away and a moment later he found himself on the banks of River Abra with the dead deer at his feet. When he examined the broken branch in his hand, he was amazed to see that the berries were agate beads. Carrying the deer on his back, he hastened home and told his wonderful story. A number of men returned with him to secure the tree. Their quest, however, was unsuccessful, for when they reached the spot, the evil spirit had taken the tree away and on the walls of the cave it had made strange carvings which can be seen even today.

# 52. The Origin of the Mole (Ukraine)

Once a rich man and a poor man owned a common field. They sowed it at the same time. The poor man's labour prospered and his seeds grew, but the rich man's seed did not grow. Out of jealousy, the rich man claimed that part of the field where the grain had sprung up. The poor man protested, but the rich man said that he should come into the field the next day for the final settlement. The poor man went home and the rich man dug a deep trench in the poor man's portion and placed his son in it saying, "When I come here tomorrow and ask whose field this is, say it is the rich man's field." Then he covered up his son with soil and went home. Next morning, when they both arrived at the field, the rich man cried, "O God! whose field is this?" "The rich man's," cried a voice from the midst of the field. But the Lord was watching everything. He revealed the truth magically and cursed the rich man's son to stay in the earth forever. The rich man's son became a mole and so the mole always hides himself from daylight.

# 53. It is Quite True (Denmark)

Once there was a hen who used to peck herself with her beak to grow more beautiful each day. With every pecking, a loose feather fell from her body. One day, two hens were talking about this habit of the bird when an owl family heard it all. They went to the

dove family and told that a hen pulled out all her feathers to look pretty to the cocks. The doves then told the pigeons about two hens that had plucked out all their feathers to attract the cock's attention. The pigeons went to the bats and told them of the three hens that died of cold as they had plucked out all their feathers. And so the story travelled and finally reached its place of origin stating that five hens had plucked out all their feathers to show which of them could best attract the cocks and then they pecked one another and died. The hen never knew that it was her own story. She said, "I despise those hens." The story was put into the newspaper; it was printed; and it's quite true that one little feather may easily become five hens.

# 54. Aunt Greenleaf and the White Deer (U.S.A.)

Aunt Greenleaf was a thin old ghostly woman. She lived in a hut surrounded by pines and sold herbal remedies to the folks in her town. People consulted her only when someone got sick because her home remedies worked too well to be natural. So, they called her a witch. The folks figured that she had to have help from the devil. Once a large pure-white deer was seen roaming in the woods at night. Many people tried to hunt it but could not catch it, so they began saying it was a phantom deer. Around that time, several misfortunes occurred in the town and the folks blamed them all on the phantom deer. There was a farmer who managed to shoot the deer with three silver bullets. The deer jerked upright and ran away. The hunter tracked it to Aunt Greenleaf's hut. The next day, the farmer learnt that Aunt Greenleaf was ill. From the moment she was ill, all the misfortunes stopped. Soon Aunt Greenleaf died and the doctor told that he found three silver bullets in her spine. After the death of Aunt Greenleaf the phantom white deer was never seen again.

# 55. Domingo's Cat (Brazil)

Once upon a time, there was a man named Domingo who was so poor that he had to sell one thing after another to get food in order to keep from starving. Finally, there was nothing left except his cat whom he loved dearly. The cat promised that Domingo would never starve as long as they were together. The cat went out into the forest, dug the soil and found many silver pieces. He took them to the king. Next day, he dug up the pieces of gold and carried them to the king. Next day, he carried the pieces of diamonds. The king asked who was sending those gifts for him. The cat replied that they were from his master Domingo. The king decided to marry his daughter to rich Domingo. He made arrangements for the wedding through the cat. The cat arranged for Domingo a beautiful palace that had one room decked with silver, one decked with gold and one decked with diamonds. A beautiful river flowed by the garden gate. Domingo and the princess were happily married but the cat was never seen again. The cat disappeared in the forest and went to make some other poor man rich.

# 56. The Entangled Mermaid (Netherlands)

Long ago, some beautiful mermaids were having a party. Just then, a young merman arrived and told the mermaids that humans had decided to turn the river into a canal and build a dyke that should keep out the ocean. All the mermaids were worried except the queen maid who doubted the merman and sent him back. After the party was over, the queen slept soon. The next morning, she noticed that the water had fallen low. She saw a dyke and fences. She was horrified and tried to clamber over the top and get through the fence. But her hair got entangled between the bars. Soon her long hair was all twisted up in the timber. When the humans saw her, they caught her and put her in a big water tank. She was put on show. She could not survive longer and finally died. Then her skin was stuffed and glass eyes put in, where her shining orbs had been. The body was mounted in the museum. So the mermaid, all because of her entanglement in the fence, was more famous when stuffed than when living, while all her young friends and older relatives were forgotten.

# 57. Black, Brown and Gray (Ireland)

One day, Fin MacCumhail chose three boys named Black, Brown and Gray to guard his castle. All three of them did their jobs sincerely. When all had risen in the morning, Fin asked them if they had any wonderful incident to tell him after the night's watching. Black told that he encountered some thieves and cleverly bought Fin's magic cup back from them. Brown told that he brought the stolen magic knife from thieves. Fin was greatly impressed with them. But Gray told that he encountered an old witch and killed her. After that her three giant sons arrived and he killed two of them but the third escaped. Fin was afraid that the third giant would bring trouble on them. One day, Fin and his companions went hunting and met a red-haired man. The man took them to a temple and fastened them to the seat. He was the third escaped giant and had come to avenge his mother and brothers' death. Fin blew a loud whistle with his mouth which was heard by his warriors. Soon they arrived and killed the giant. All were happy and they returned to the castle.

# 58. The White Maiden (Germany)

Once during the noon of a mid-summer day, a young noble was hunting in a valley. He was tired after chasing his game and sat in the shadow of an old abandoned castle. He wished he could have some wine. Just then, a beautiful maiden appeared before him from the castle. She was bearing in her hands a huge silver beaker of antique form, full of wine. She was fair with long hair and loving eyes. The young noble fell in love with her just at the first sight. She offered him the wine. He drank it all. After this, she disappeared into the castle. The young noble rushed inside the castle but it was all ivy-covered and neither the maiden nor any other living soul was there inside. He returned back disappointed. Since then, he always remained sad. Again and again, he visited the castle but never found the maiden. Grief-stricken and feeble, he once lay at the entrance of the castle when the maiden once again appeared before him. He stretched forth his hands and they both hugged each other. The white maiden and the noble were never seen again.

# 59. The Old Man and His Rooster (Rome)

There was once an old couple. The husband owned a rooster while his wife owned a hen. The hen laid many eggs but the old woman never gave any egg to her husband saying that he should beat his rooster so that he might lay eggs for him. The old man gave his rooster a sound thrashing hoping to get some eggs. But the rooster was unable to bear the thrashing, so he ran away. But someone caught him and put him in his treasure box. The rooster swallowed all the gold coins from his treasury and escaped. He came back to the old man and shook out a pile of gold coins. The old man, in his delight, kissed the rooster. When his wife saw the gold coins, she asked her husband to give her a few gold coins. But the old man refused to give any saying that she should beat her hen so that she might bring gold coins for her. The old woman soon began to beat her hen. She beat her till she was dead. So the old woman remained poor while the old man became very rich.

# 60. Mr. Vinegar (England)

Once there lived Mr. and Mrs. Vinegar in a glass bottle. One day, when Mr. Vinegar was away from home, Mrs. Vinegar was busy sweeping her house, when an unlucky thump of the broom broke the vinegar bottle. In an agony of grief, she rushed to meet her husband and told him what had happened. The couple then went to a thick forest. They both were tired and fell asleep. Next morning, they found a number of gold coins. Using them, Mr. Vinegar bought a cow so that Mrs. Vinegar might make butter and cheese, which he should sell in the market and they could live comfortably. But on his way, he saw that a bagpiper was making good money by playing his bagpipe. Mr. Vinegar greedily exchanged his cow for the bagpipe. But when he tried to play a tune, people laughed at him instead of giving him money. His fingers grew very cold and so he exchanged his bagpipe for a pair of gloves. At last, he grew very tired while travelling back to his wife. He had to exchange his gloves with a walking stick and returned to his wife empty-handed.

# 61. Why Flies Bother Cows (Nigeria)

The Queen of Calabar used to give big feasts to all the domestic animals but never invited the wild beasts. At one feast, there were three large tables and she told the cow to sit at the head of the table and share out the food. The first course was passed, which the cow shared out amongst the people. But the cow forgot the tiny fly who himself called out to the cow to give him his share, but the cow said, "Be quiet; you must have patience." When the second course arrived, the fly again called out to the cow, but the cow told the fly that he would get food later. At last all the dishes were finished and the fly was given no supper by the cow. Next day, the fly complained to the queen, who decided that, as the cow had presided at the feast and had not given the fly his share, in the future the fly could always get his food from the cow's eyes wherever she went. So, even at the present time, wherever cows are, flies can always be seen feeding off their eyes in accordance with the queen's orders.

# 62. The Painter and the Wood-Carver (Arabia)

Once there lived a painter and a wood-carver. They hated each other. Once the painter told the Badshah that his father had always wished to construct a pagoda in heaven, so the Badshah must send a skilled wood-carver up to heaven. The badshah called the wood-carver and told him the matter. The wood-carver knew that it was the painter's trick. He secretly built a passage, from his own house into the middle of his field. Over the opening in the field he placed a large stone. Soon by the Badshah's orders, the wood-carver was put to fire in a faggot with all his tools. But he escaped by the covered way he had made back to his own house. Everybody thought that the wood-carver had gone to heaven. However, he remained concealed at home during the whole month. After that, he went back to the Badshah and told that he had completed his work and for the decoration of the pagoda Badshah's father had asked to send a painter. Once again, in the midst of the field, a pile of faggots was kindled and the painter was burnt into it. Thus, the wood-carver took his revenge.

# 63. Goat-Face (Italy)

Once there was a giant green lizard. She took a poor peasant's daughter in exchange of a bag full of gold. The peasant was happy. The lizard, who was a fairy in disguise, made a beautiful palace for her new daughter and put a hundred maidens to her service. But her daughter was always ungrateful towards her. Once a king saw her daughter and fell in love with her. The lizard arranged their wedding with marvellous arrangements. But the daughter did not express any gratitude towards her mother. Instead, she cursed that her face should become that of a goat. Now, the king began disliking her. Instead of loving her as his queen, he put her as a maid in the palace kitchen. The rude, unmannerly and thankless girl having little gratitude had brought the quarrel on herself. She went to her mother, threw herself at her feet and asked pardon for the ill-treatment. The fairy embraced, kissed her and restored her to former appearance. When the king beheld her, so beautiful and splendidly attired, he started loving her as his wife. Thus, she lived happliy, loving her husband and honouring her mother.

# 64. The Cat on the Dovrefell (Norway)

Once there was a man who had a great grey-white bear, which he was going to take to the king. He came to the Dovrefell and saw a cottage where an old man lived. He asked the old man if he could get a room there for his bear and himself. The old man refused saying that every night, trolls came to his small cottage to trouble him. So, he couldn't shelter anyone. The man with the bear promised to help the old man and so he got leave to stay there. When the trolls arrived, the bear lay under the stove. A small troll took a piece of sausage, stuck it on a fork and poked it up against the bear's nose. The white bear rose up and growled, and hunted all the trolls out of door. After some months, when the old man was cutting wood, a troll arrived and asked if the old man still had his big cat. The old man told that she still lay under the stove and had got seven kittens, far bigger and fiercer than the cat. Frightened, the troll ran away in the wood and never troubled the old man again.

# 65. The Silver Saucer and the Transparent Apple (Russia)

Once there was a merchant who had three daughters. One day the merchant asked his daughters what they wanted him to gift them. The eldest demanded for a necklace while the second asked for a new dress. But the youngest asked for a silver saucer and a transparent apple. The merchant fulfilled their demands. The youngest sat down spinning the apple in the saucer and surprisingly saw the happenings of the whole world. Her sisters took her to the forest and killed her out of jealousy. They buried her under a tree. Many years later, a reed grew from where the girl was buried. A peasant made a whistle pipe out of the reed. When he played the pipe, a song was heard that narrated the story of the girl's murder. The story reached the merchant and he soon found her dead daughter buried under the tree. He went to the Tzar, little father of all good Russians, and took a glass of water from his well and poured it on her dead daughter. She became alive. She forgave her sisters. She was made Tzaritza, a kind mother to Holy Russia and the wife of Tzar.

# 66. The Zebra Stallion (South Africa)

Once in the dense forests of South Africa, a baboon used to disturb the zebra mares. He would not let them drink water when they arrived at the river to quench their thirst. Once a mare gave birth to a foal. Other mares helped her to suckle the young foal. He grew up to be a big strong stallion. One day, when the mares were thirsty, the stallion brought them to the river to drink water. Seeing the zebra mares at the river, the baboon came to trouble them as he formerly used to do. All mares were worried and in great need of water. Seeing their inconvenience, the

stallion stepped forward. He was angry for the baboon's misbehaviour with his mother and other elder members of his family and his herd. He took the baboon by his shoulders, and pressed him upon a hot, flat rock. Since that day each of the baboons had bald place on back. Frightened, the baboon ran away and never troubled the zebra mares again. He lamented over his action but it was now too late for repentance. He, being a gum-eater, was outdone by a milk-eater.

# 67. A Beautiful Lady Saved the King (Taiwan)

Thousands of years ago, there was a country that was ruled by another country. The king was a slave who worked for the foreign ruler of this country. His staff officer was trying to save the king and his country. While the staff officer was walking along the river, he saw a beautiful lady washing clothes. He thought maybe because she was so beautiful, the foreign ruler would fall in love with her. So, he sent her to the palace. Once she was there, the foreign ruler fell in love with her and did not care about anything else, not even ruling the country. So, the lady and the staff officer saved their king and their country. In the end, they went away with their king and lived together at a place none knew. If the lady had not been beautiful, the staff officer would not have sent her into the palace, and the foreign ruler would not have fallen in love with her. If the ruler had not fallen in love with her, they would not have been able to save their country. So, beauty is important.

# 68. The Greedy Farmer (Turkey)

Once there lived a farmer in a village. He was very ambitious. He wanted to make more and more money. In spring, when it was rainy, he called out to God, " If it were sunny, I would have sown some wheat." Next day, it became sunny, and the farmer sowed some wheat. After that, he called out to God, " If it were rainy, it would have been greatly useful for my wheat." The following day, it rained heavily. The farmer called out to God, "If you had given more rain, my wheat would have grown even more." The following day, it rained again, much heavily than the previous day. Then, in summer, the farmer harvested his wheat and collected it in a heap. The farmer called out to God, " If you had given more rain, my wheat harvest would have been bigger." He angrily asked God, " Why didn't you give me more rain to produce more wheat?" God turned very angry on him. Out of rage, He sent down heavy rain and stormy winds and all the wheat of the farmer floated away with the water.

# 69. The Prince and the Princess (Lebanon)

A long time ago, there was a prince who was very brave and a great knight. There was a princess too who was very beautiful and kind. They loved each other and lived happily in a big castle. One day a witch went to the castle and said to them, "I hate you both as I hate to love. I am going to kill you." "No, I will kill you," the prince replied bravely. Then, the prince tried to kill the witch, but he was not able to do anything because he was changed into a fox as soon as the witch said, "Prince, change into a fox." Then, the princess tried to help her love, but the witch changed her into a frog. After that, the witch took them to a prison in a tower. After a few days, someone sent a dragon to help the prisoners. The dragon went to the witch and blew some fire from his mouth and burnt her. After the witch was killed by the dragon, the prince and the princess returned to their natural selves and lived happily together for the rest of their life.

# 70. Outwitting A Crocodile (Malaysia)

Sang Kancil was a clever deer. He lived along a river. Sang Buaya was a big bad crocodile who lived in the river with other crocodiles. They had always wished to catch Sang Kancil and eat him. But never had they succeeded in doing so because of Sang Kancil's tricks. One day, when Sang Kancil was walking along the river, he saw some delicious fruits on the trees on the other side of the river. But he could not cross the river and thought of an idea. He called out to Sang Buaya who slowly came out of the water. Sang Kancil told him that the king was having a big feast with lots of food and he was inviting everyone, including him and all the other crocodiles. So, he needed to know how many crocodiles would come. Soon, all the crocodiles came and made a line across the river. Sang Kancil then stepped on each crocodile, counting each one and finally crossed the river. He then thanked Sang Buaya for his help. All the crocodiles were shocked and felt embarrassed at being tricked by Sang Kancil again who was enjoying tasty fruits because of them.

# 71. Endless Love (Korea)

Once there was a couple, Soo-il and Soon-ae, who loved each other so much. But Soon-ae's rich father never allowed her to marry poor Soo-il. According to his own will, he forcefully married her to Jung-bae. But she was unhappy because her husband hung out with friends and seldom came home. One day, Soon-ae saw Soo-il standing at her window. She jumped down from her room, which was on the second floor and fainted. When she opened her eyes, she was surrounded by her family. She discovered that she could not move at all and was upset. Her father would not let Soo-ill see Soon-ae. So, they secretly moved to a town where none could find them. There, Soon-ae slowly recovered. One day Soo-il went to pluck a rose on the edge of a cliff but he slid and fell over the cliff. When Soon-ae heard this, she went to the cliff but could only find a strange flower. After a week, she too died of grief and was buried near the place where the flower was found. After a while, another flower appeared in the same place as the first one.

# 72. The Old Man and the Golden Fish (China)

One day, an old man went out fishing in a lake at night. After a while, he fell asleep in his boat. He woke up suddenly as his fishing rod was shaking. He pulled up the rod. He was amazed at the sight of a golden fish who could talk to him like humans. She gave the old man a golden rope and begged him to let her go. The man was very happy and took the rope greedily from the fish. But he did not let the fish go. "Let me go now as you have the golden rope," said the fish. "No, I will never let you go. I am going to sell you. I think someone will pay a very high price to get a talking golden fish like you," the old man said. The man then put the fish into a container, which was full of water and continued to row towards his home. But soon his boat began to sink into the lake and finally it sank completely into the lake. The old man died because of his greed and the golden fish happily swam back into the lake.

# 73. Finbo (Sri Lanka)

Once in a deep blue ocean, there lived a little blue whale named Finbo. He loved playing hide-and-seek with his friends but he always ended up being on the losing end. He never succeeded in hiding himself due to his large size. This made Finbo upset. He hated himself for being so large. His friends made fun of his giant size. His mother always told him the benefits and their uniqueness of being so big but he was never convinced. One day, Finbo and his friends went to the rocky area to play hide-and-seek. They went far away, beyond the rocky area. But Finbo did not accompany them as his mother had told him that it was dangerous there. After sometime, he heard the shrieking voices of his friends. He swam towards them and saw that a big shark was racing towards them with his mouth wide open. On seeing Finbo, they rushed towards him and hid behind his tail. When the shark saw the big blue Finbo, it ran away, frightened. All the friends were very proud of Finbo. He told them that being brave does not mean running towards danger.

# 74. The Frog's Skin (Georgia)

Once there were three brothers who decided to take their wives from the place where their arrows would fall after being shot from their bows. They shot their arrows. The arrows of the two elder brothers fell on noblemen's houses, so they led home their noble wives. The youngest brother's arrow fell into a lake, so he married a frog that was croaking. But his brothers did not like this and threw him out of the house with his frog. He started living in a small cottage where the frog took off the frog's skin and turned to a beautiful maiden. The boy seized the frog's skin and burnt it. Soon the news spread to the whole countryside that the man possessed a lovely woman who had come to him from heaven.

When the lord of the country heard of this, he threatened the boy that he would be killed if he did not give him his wife. The boy sought the help of the lord's mother in heaven who gave him a casket. The boy took the casket to the lord. The lord opened the casket and there came forth fire, which swallowed him up.

# 75. The She-Wolf (Croatia)

There was an enchanted mill; a she-wolf always haunted it. A soldier went once into the mill to sleep. Just then, the she-wolf came in to look about the mill to see whether she could find anything to eat but found nothing. She shed off her wolf skin and turned into a damsel and slept there. The soldier nailed fast the skin to the mill-wheel. He met the damsel and proposed her to marry him. Not able to find her skin, the damsel agreed to marry the soldier. They soon married and had a son. One day, the son went to the fields along with his father. He told his father that he had heard that her mother was a wolf. He asked if it was true. His father replied that it was true and showed him her skin on the mill-wheel. On reaching home, he at once said to his mother, "Mamma! You are a wolf! I saw your skin." His mother asked him, "Where is my skin?" He said, "There, on the mill-wheel." His mother thanked his son for rescuing her. Then she went away and was never seen again.

# 76. Green Beard (Lithuania)

Once in a city, there lived a very wealthy merchant. He had a very beautiful daughter who wished to marry a man who possessed green beard. In the forests near the city, lived twenty-four robbers. Their captain dyed his beard green. On listening the girl's desire he then went to marry the merchant's daughter. The girl liked him and his green beard, and their marriage was fixed. Before wedding, he invited her to his great mansion in the forest. Next day, she went into the forest and found no mansion but only a small house with two lions chained near the door. She went inside and saw a little bird in a cage who told her that the robbers were human-eaters. So, she lay down under the bed. When the robbers came home and fell asleep, she escaped. The lions began to roar loudly and awakened the robbers. But the girl reached home safely. Next day, the robbers went again to rob the merchant and kidnap his daughter. But the merchant's men captured them all and put in prison. The girl no longer showed any desire for green beard.

# 77. The Dog and the Wolf (Bohemia)

There was a peasant family who had a house dog named Sultan. When Sultan grew old, the peasant drove him away, thinking that he was no longer of any use to his family. Sadly, he wandered about and reached a forest. He encountered a wolf that intended to eat him. Sultan suggested that the wolf should feed the dog first and gobble him when he became fattened. The wolf agreed and fed him well for many days till Sultan was strong enough to take up the cudgels with him. The wolf himself ate a little to feed the dog best, so Sultan gained in flesh and strength, while the wolf equally fell off. When the wolf tried to eat Sultan, he made a bold dash and the wolf lay on the ground overcome by Sultan. Then in one spring the dog held the wolf by the throat and put an end to him. The news of Sultan's heroic deeds spread far and wide, even to that village where Sultan had formerly served. The consequence was that the peasant family took back again their faithful house dog and lovingly cared for him.

# 78. The Sagacious Monkey and the Boar (Japan)

Once there lived a monkey man in Japan who earned his living by taking round a monkey and showing off the animal's tricks. When his monkey became old, he began forgetting his tricks. Not even his master's harsh beating could make him dance and perform properly. The man decided to sell him to a butcher. When the monkey came to know about this, he went to the wise wild boar in the forest and told him his tale of woe. They both made a plan and the monkey went home happy and excited. Next morning, the master's wife began her household work and placed her child near the porch. Suddenly, the boar took her child in its clutch and disappeared through the gate. The monkey ran after the thief as hard as his legs would carry him. The couple's gratitude knew no bounds when the faithful monkey brought the child safely back to their arms. The man gave up his thought of selling the monkey to the butcher. The monkey was patted and lived the rest of his days in peace. His master never beat him again even though he did not perform his tricks well.

# 79. How Saint Peter Lost His Hair (Germany)

Saint Peter was entirely bald, except for a single lock of hair that fell over his forehead. Once, while he and Lord Christ were travelling together, they came to a farmhouse where a woman was just cooking up some large yeast pancakes in grease. Saint Peter entered the house to beg for some pancakes, while the Lord waited outside. The woman gave Peter three pancakes. But Peter was selfish. When the pancakes were divided up, he quickly hid one of them in his cap, then put it on his head. He pretended that he had received only two pancakes, one of which he gave to the Lord. The pancake under his cap was still hot, and it began to burn Peter terribly on the head, but he could not do anything about it; he just had to bear the pain. Later, when he took off his cap, he discovered that the hot pancake had burnt into his head a large bald spot, which remained with him as long as he lived. Only the lock of hair that had protruded from the front of his cap was spared. Thus Saint Peter's bald head had one lock of hair in front.

# 80. The Devil as Partner (Switzerland)

Once a journeyman stayed in an inn for many days. When the innkeeper asked for the bill, he told that he would pay the bill the next day because he did not have enough money. After a while, a black devil appeared before the journeyman and asked him to stay in the inn for seven years. He promised to keep him out of debt and provide all that he wanted but asked him not to wash himself, nor to comb or cut his hair or nails. The journeyman agreed. The journeyman stayed at the inn for many years paying all his bills. But he had become wild in appearance because of his dirty body, long and dirty hair and nails. One day, a merchant friend of the innkeeper badly miscalculated in a business deal and could not get out of the difficulty. The innkeeper took him to the journeyman who agreed to pay the merchant's debts if he married his daughter to the journeyman. The merchant agreed and the wedding occurred in a church when the journeyman turned into a handsome nobleman. He thanked the devil for being his partner.

# 81. A friend in Need is a Friend Indeed (England)

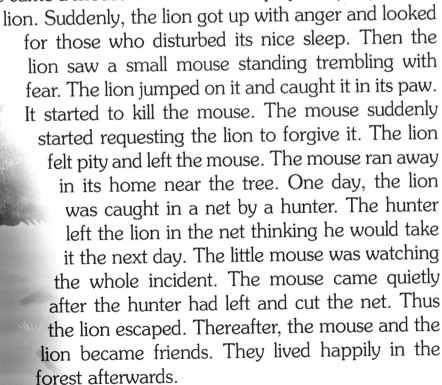

Once upon a time, there lived a lion in a forest. One day after a heavy meal, it was sleeping under a tree. After sometime, there came a mouse and it started to play and jump on the lion. Suddenly, the lion got up with anger and looked for those who disturbed its nice sleep. Then the lion saw a small mouse standing trembling with fear. The lion jumped on it and caught it in its paw. It started to kill the mouse. The mouse suddenly started requesting the lion to forgive it. The lion felt pity and left the mouse. The mouse ran away in its home near the tree. One day, the lion was caught in a net by a hunter. The hunter left the lion in the net thinking he would take it the next day. The little mouse was watching the whole incident. The mouse came quietly after the hunter had left and cut the net. Thus the lion escaped. Thereafter, the mouse and the lion became friends. They lived happily in the forest afterwards.

# 82. The Town Mouse and the Country Mouse (Tasmania)

A Town Mouse and a Country Mouse were friends. The Country Mouse invited his friend to come and see him at his home in the fields. The Town Mouse came and they sat down for a dinner of barley, corns and roots. The flavour was not much to the taste of the guest and he said, "My poor dear friend, you live here no better than the ants. You must come and stay with me." So when he returned to the town, he took the Country Mouse with him and showed him into a larder containing flour, oatmeal, figs, honey and dates. The Country Mouse had never seen anything like it and sat down to enjoy the luxuries his friend provided. But before they could begin, the door of the larder opened and someone came in. The two mice scampered off and hid themselves in a narrow and exceedingly uncomfortable hole. When all was quiet, they ventured out again. It was too much. The Country Mouse said, "Good bye. You live in the lap of luxury; I can see, but you are surrounded by dangers whereas at my home I can enjoy simple dinner of roots and corn in peace."

# 83. Pandora Box (Greece)

One day, the god created a beautiful woman called Pandora and took her to Prometheus. His brother, Epimetheus, married her. The couple lived happily together until one day Mercury, the messenger of the gods, arrived with a mysterious box. He asked Pandora and her husband to take care of it. He made them promise never to look inside it. For days Pandora could not take her eyes off the box. All the time she wondered what was

inside. One day, she slowly lifted the lid and looked inside. To her surprise, there were no glittering jewels, dresses, golden coins–instead the god had filled the box with all evils now known to mankind. Disease, misery and death buzzed around stinging her. Pandora screamed and screamed with pain and fear. Epimetheus heard her cries as he ran towards her. Pandora and Epimetheus heard a little voice coming from the box. 'Let me out!' Believing that nothing inside the box could be worse than the horrors released, they opened the lid once more. All that remained was a butterfly. The beautiful butterfly was–hope, which Mercury had hidden amongst the evils.

# 84. The Galah, and Oolah the Lizard (Australia)

Oolah the lizard was tired of lying in the sun, doing nothing. He took his boomerangs out, and began to practise throwing them. While he was doing so, a Galah came up, and stood near, watching the boomerangs come flying back. Oolah was proud of having the Galah to watch his skill. The boomerang hit the Galah on the top of her head, taking both feathers and skin clean off. Oolah was frightened when blood started coming out of the Galah's head. He glided away to hide under a bindeah bush. The Galah followed Oolah. She caught him and made a hole in his skin. Then, she rubbed his skin with her own bleeding head. "Now then," she said, "you Oolah shall carry bindeahs on you always and the stain of my blood." "And you," said Oolah, as he hissed with pain from the tingling of the prickles, "shall be a bald-headed bird as long as I am a red prickly lizard." So to this day, underneath the Galah's crest you can always find the bald patch which the bubberah of Oolah first made. And in the country of the Galahs are lizards coloured reddish-brown, and covered with spikes like bindeah prickles.

# 85. The Man Who Never Lied (Africa)

Once upon a time, there lived a wise man by the name of Mamad. He never lied. The king ordered his subjects to bring him to the palace. The king was about to leave for the forest. The king held his horse by the mane; his left foot was already on the stirrup. He ordered Mamad, "Tell the queen I will be with her for lunch. You will have lunch with me then." Mamad went to the queen. Then the king laughed and said, "We won't go hunting and now Mamad will lie to the queen." But wise Mamad went to the palace and said, "Maybe you should prepare a big feast for lunch tomorrow, and maybe you shouldn't. Maybe the king will come by noon, and maybe he won't." "Tell me weather he will come, or not," asked the queen. "I don't know whether he put his right foot on the stirrup, or he put his left foot on the ground after I had left." The king came the next day and said to the queen, "The wise Mamad lied to you yesterday." But the queen told him about the words of Mamad. And the king realized that the wise man never lied.

# 86. The Boy Who Cried Wolf (Britain)

A shepherd-boy lived in a small village. He watched a flock of sheep near a village. He used to call out the villagers three or four times by saying out, "Wolf! Wolf!" and when his neighbours came to help him, he always used to laugh at them for their pain and foolishness. And it had become a joke in the village. But one day as fate had it, the Wolf truly came. The shepherd-boy, now really alarmed, shouted in an agony of terror, "Please do come and help me; the wolf is killing the sheep." But none paid any heed to his cries, nor rendered any assistance. The wolf, having no cause of fear, at his leisure destroyed the whole flock. The boy kept shouting for help but everyone thought this time also he was lying. The boy had paid for being dishonest and troubling everyone with his pranks. There is no one believing a liar, even when he speaks the truth. We should never befool people. We cannot befool them all the time.

# 87. The Fairy and the Old Woman (North America)

Once upon a time, there was a good old woman who lived in a little house. She had in her garden a bed of beautiful striped tulips. One night, the old woman looked closely and she saw, standing by each tulip, a little Fairy mother who was crooning and rocking the flower like a cradle, while in each tulip-cup lay a little Fairy baby laughing and playing. The good old woman stole quietly back to her house and from that time on she never picked a tulip, nor allowed her neighbours to touch the flowers. The tulips grew daily brighter in colour and larger in size and gave out a delicious perfume like that of roses. They began to bloom all the year round too. The day came when the good old woman died and the tulip-bed was torn up by folks. Parsley was planted there instead of the flowers. But parsley along with all the other plants in the garden, and from that time nothing would grow there. But the good old woman's grave grew beautiful, for the fairies sang above it, and kept it green.

# 88. Two Frogs (Berlin)

Two frogs had lived in a village all throughout their life. They thought they would like to go and see the big city that was about ten miles away. They talked about it for a long time and at last they set off to see the city. It was a hot day and they soon began to feel tired. They had only gone a little way when one said to the other, "We must be nearly there. Can you see the city?" "No," said the other frog, "but if I climb on your back I might be able to see it." So, he climbed up on the back of the other frog to see the city. Now when the frog put up his head, his eyes could only see what was behind, and not what was in front. So, he saw the village they had just left. "Can you see the city?" asked the frog who was below. "Yes," answered the frog that had climbed up, "I can see it. It looks just like our village." Then the frogs went back and told the frogs round the village that they had seen the city and it was just like theirs.

# 89. The Crocodile (Russia)

There was once a baby crocodile. He had a beautiful shiny tail and all the other crocodiles were horrible to him because they were jealous of him. One day the baby crocodile counted all his beautiful shiny scales and there were a thousand, a lot more than he thought. So, he counted all the other crocodiles and there were twenty and that was including the grown-up crocodiles. He decided that he had many scales and could spare forty from his tummy, so he wished for forty of his scales to be on his pillow by morning, but there weren't any. Even three weeks later, there weren't any. Then one day, a magic

crocodile granted him a wish. He wished for forty of his scales to be on his pillow when he woke up in the morning. He woke up and there were forty beautiful shiny scales on his pillow. So, he gave all twenty crocodiles, including his parents two scales each. From then on everybody was kind to the baby crocodile who had given away forty of his beautiful shiny scales.

# 90. A Hard Decision (Siberia)

There was a Siberian husky; her name was Siberia. She had two friends. One was a Chihuahua; her name was Chichi. Her other friend was a Golden Retriever; her name was Goldie. She had fun with her friends. One day, Siberia and Goldie were going for a walk; Chichi came by. She saw them walking together. Chichi didn't like that. Chichi pushed Goldie in the bush. Siberia barked, "Stop." Goldie liked Chichi as a friend, but Chichi didn't. Goldie was injured in the bush. Siberia asked, "Why did you push Goldie?" Chichi said, "I don't like Goldie; she is mean to me so I don't want you to hang out with her." Siberia invited them over to her house but they wouldn't know that the other person was coming. Siberia invited them to dinner. One came from the back door and the other from the front. Siberia sat them down. Chichi said, "What is Goldie doing here?" "I invited you both over," said Siberia. They kept on fighting and fighting. Siberia was surprised that they got along with each other in due course. So, they went on lots of trips together and never fought again. They were friends forever.

# 91. Birthday Bike (America)

Michael's birthday was coming soon, so he asked his dad for a bicycle so that he might not need to walk to school any more. Michael got a book instead but he did not complain. One day, Michael saw a big boy named William on a bike. As the boy was turning around a corner, the bike skidded on a puddle of water and crashed into a lamp-post. The boy was

a prefect in Michael's school. William seemed to have broken his leg. Michael picked William's bike up. It was not damaged; he took him to the nearby hospital. After school, Michael quickly rode the bicycle to William's house with a book and a jigsaw puzzle for William. William was not too seriously hurt. He was discharged after his leg was put in a cast. To Michael's surprise, William was getting a new bike on his birthday in two months' time and Michael could have William's old bike. Michael was overjoyed. From then on, Michael and William became good friends. Michael visited William every day till William's leg was healed.

# 92. The Blind Boy (Britain)

Early morning many people were busy rushing to their office on time. A blind boy sat on the steps of a building with a hat by his feet. He held up a sign which said, "I am blind please help." There were only a few coins in the hat. A man was walking by the boy. He took a few coins from his pocket and dropped into the hat. He then took the sign, turned it around, and wrote some words. He put the sign back so that everyone who walked by might see the new words. Soon the hat began to fill up. A lot more people were giving money to the blind boy. That afternoon, the man who had changed the sign came to see how things were. The boy recognized his footsteps and asked, "Were you the one who changed my sign this morning? What did you write?" The man said, "I only wrote the truth. I said what you said but in a different way." What he had written was: "Today is a beautiful day and I cannot see it."

# 93. The Culprit (India)

Once there lived a culprit by the name of Poornananda in a village far away. He had two disciples–Nagendra and Krishna. One day while the two were coming to the village from the city, Naga (Nagendra's nickname) picked a fight with a horse-cart driver. The fight

reached a flashpoint and Naga unable to control himself any longer, slapped the horse-cart driver. The driver fell down. Feeling ashamed of himself, after hearing his guru's words, Naga fell at his feet and begged forgiveness. But Krishna was watching all this with glee. "Naga was a big bully. It's good that you came along, guru. This incident is a shame even to me," Krishna said. On hearing this Poornananda's face turned red. He told, "One is a big bully. But what about the other bully ? Quietly watching the fight with glee! So you, too, are equally guilty." Krishna hung his head in shame.

# 94. The Greedy Mouse (India)

A greedy mouse saw a basket full of corn. He wanted to eat it. So he made a small hole in the basket. He squeezed in through the hole. He ate a lot of corn. He felt full and was very happy. Now he wanted to come out. He tried to come out through the small hole but could not. His belly was full. He tried again but it was of no use. The mouse started crying. A rabbit was passing by. It heard the mouse's cry and asked, "Why are you crying, my friend?" The mouse explained, "I made a small hole and entered into the basket. Now I am not able to get out through that hole." The rabbit said, "It is because you ate too much. Wait till your belly shrinks." The rabbit laughed and went away. The mouse fell asleep in the basket. Next morning, his belly had shrunk. But the mouse wanted to eat some corn. So he ate and ate. His belly was full once again. He thought, 'Oh! Now I will go out tomorrow.' The cat was the next passer-by. He smelt the mouse in the basket. He lifted its lid and ate the mouse.

# 95. Suchimukha and the Monkey (India)

A gang of monkeys made their home in a mountain slope. When winter came, it brought not only severe cold but also heavy rains. Unable to stand the cold, the monkeys collected red berries growing in the mountain slope. They gathered around the berries and began blowing air at them thinking they were embers. Watching their vain effort in amusement, Suchimukha, a bird, told them, "You fool, they are not embers but red berries. Why do you waste your energy on them? This will not save you from cold. Go and look for a shelter in a cave or a place free from wind. The clouds are thick and there will be no immediate relief from rain." An old member of the monkey gang angrily told the bird, "Why do you poke your nose in our affairs? Go away." Disregarding the old monkey's anger and not giving room to any other monkey to talk, Suchimukha went on repeating his advice to them to seek shelter elsewhere. Tired with the bird's unwanted advice, one of the monkeys sprang at the bird and bashed him against a rock till he was dead.

# 96. The Nightingale (Europe)

One day a nobleman caught a nightingale and wanted to put it in a cage. But the bird spoke to him, "Let me go and I will give you three pieces of good advice. It may be of use to you some day." The nobleman agreed to let it go. The nightingale gave him three pieces of advice, "Never be sorry for something that cannot be brought back, my lord. And never trust idle words." The nobleman heard the advice and let the nightingale go. The bird flew out and said, "Too bad; you let me go. If only you knew about my treasure. I have a very huge expensive gem under my wing. If you had taken it, you would have become even richer. When the nobleman heard that he began to regret letting bitterly about the bird go. The nightingale turned towards him and said, "Now I know, master, that you are a greedy and foolish man. You were sorry for something that cannot be brought back. And you believed my idle words. Look at what a little bird I am. How could I be hiding a large gem under my wing?" And after these words the bird flew away.

# 97. From White to Black (Japan)

In those days when the world was new and young, the crow used to be of white colour with stylish feathers curled at ends. Once he went to an owl, who was dexterously known for his art of painting and urged the owl to colour him with very fine and unique colour. The owl led his customer into the dyeing room and put him into a pot of indigo. When the crow was taken out, the ends of his feathers had straightened out and he was glossy black. The crow was furious. The owl reminded him that he had asked to be dyed in a unique colour but the crow refused to listen and gave the owl a vicious peck. The owl abandoned his business and fled. Since that day, the owl was habituated to escape from his infuriated friends and began to come out only at night to avoid the wrath of his dissatisfied customer.

# 98. Lightning and Thunder (Nigeria)

In the olden days, thunder and lightning lived on the earth amongst all the other people. But the king made them live at the far end of the town as far as possible from other people's houses. Thunder was an old mother and lightning was her son, a ram. Whenever the ram got angry, he used to go about and burn houses and knock down trees. He even did damage on the farms. Whenever Ram did these things, his mother used to call out to him in a very loud voice to stop and not to do any more damage when he was in a bad temper, he used to do despread damage. At last, the people could not stand it any longer and complained to the king. They requested the king to banish both lightning and thunder from the earth and make them live in the sky where they could not cause so much destruction. Ever since, when lightning is angry, it commits damage as before, but you can hear his mother, thunder, rebuking him and telling him to stop.

# 99. The Herb 'Mega' (Asia)

A poor merchant dropped in a village inn to spend the night. He left aside his merchandise and asked the innkeeper to prepare dinner. The merchant had a few items and a couple of coins, but the greedy innkeeper thought, 'Why shouldn't I take all his merchandise and

money.' "There's nothing easier than that," said the innkeeper's husband, "Just put some of the herb named 'mega' in his meal. Everyone who eats the herb forgets something." She put the herb in the merchant's dinner. He ate the meal, thanked the innkeeper and went to bed. The merchant left the inn in early the following morning. When the innkeeper woke up, she went to the merchant's room immediately. But the room was empty. She started to scream at her husband, "What foolishness have you told me about this herb? The merchant forgot nothing." "Then he must have forgotten something else!" said the husband. The innkeeper started thinking, 'What could have the merchant forgotten?' Suddenly she slapped herself on the forehead and said, "He forgot to pay, you old fool!"

# 100. The Little Fish and the Big Fat Bean (Ukraine)

One day, a little fish was out swimming in the river with her mother. The water was clear and warm. The little fish wanted to swim faster and go farther. So, she swam on and on till she reached the riverbank. She looked, and there, growing on the bank, she saw a large bean stalk and on the bean stalk, a big, fat bean. The little fish thought that she had never seen anything so funny. "Hullo there, Fatso!" she called to the bean. "Hullo, Midge!" the bean called back. The little fish felt very hurt when she was called in that manner. She burst into tears and hurried off to complain to her mother about it. "Perhaps you hurt the bean's feelings yourself in some way," said the mother fish." "Oh, no, mother dear, I didn't!" "Well, let's swim back to the bank again and I'll ask the bean what made him say such a thing." "Tell me, Mr. Bean, what made you hurt my little daughter's feelings? Why did you call her Midge?" "She only got as good as she gave. She called me Fatso, so I called her Midge in return!"

# 101. The Prince (France)

Once there was a king who did justice to all his subjects. The king had a son who got good education of arts and science. Everyone asked the prince something. He promised this and that, and then he forgot his promises the next day. For this reason, it was

not surprising that even his friends did not attach much importance to his words. One day, the prince and his friends were playing on the bank of a river. They jumped on a rocky promontory in fresh waves. The previous day, there had been a lot of rain and the river was in spate. The current was very dangerous. This did not prevent the prince away from the bank because he wanted to prove his fearlessness. But the current was too strong. He dived into the water. He called aloud for help but his friends did not acknowledge the point of danger. Maybe they thought he would laugh at them. None ever saw him again.

## 102. The Blue Smurf (Belgium)

John liked to take care of his garden and clean the statues of elfs and smurfs. He saw something strange one day. The ceramic figure of the blue smurf was outside beside the other statues. He ran to the wood house to check it. When he came in, he saw that the smurf that he had seen before was not there any more. He was really surprised and thought that maybe somebody was tricking him. John wanted to discover. "Don't be afraid, John. All the blue smurfs are alive, but we just move and talk when nobody is watching. I did not want to be at the wood house, so I came here to be with my family. Can I be here?" asked the blue smurf. John thought he was dreaming and all the smurfs started moving; it was real."Sorry blue smurf; I did not want to separate you from your family. Of course, you can stay at the garden," said John excited. That is how John discovered the secret of his garden. The blue smurfs were alive and they were taking care of his garden.

## 103. The Proud Red Rose (Pakistan)

One beautiful spring day, a red rose blossomed in a forest. Many kinds of trees and plants grew there. As the rose looked around, a pine tree near by said, "What a beautiful flower! I wish I would be that lovely." Another tree said, "Dear pine, do not be sad; we cannot have everything." The rose turned its head and remarked, "It seems that I am the most beautiful plant in this forest." A sunflower raised its yellow head and asked, "Why do you say that? In this forest, there are many beautiful plants. You are just one of them." The red rose replied, "I see everyone looking at me and admiring me." Then the rose looked at a cactus and said, "Look at that ugly plant full of thorns!" The pine tree said, "Red rose, what kind of talk is this? Who can say what beauty is? You have thorns too." The proud red rose looked angrily at the pine and said, "I thought you had good taste! You do not know what beauty is at all. You cannot compare my thorns to those of the cactus."

# 104. Christmas Surprise (America)

It was two days before Christmas. Harry, Cornelius, Monty and I were busy building a snowman when Fritz appeared with his little niece Emily and introduced her. "Emily is from the South and has never seen snow before," Fritz told us, "She doesn't know much about our winters." It turned out that Emily didn't know much about Christmas. "Who is Santa Claus, Waldo?" she asked me, shivering in the cold air. "Santa Claus," I explained, "brings presents and toys to human children at Christmas time." "Does he also bring presents to animal children?" Emily asked. "Well," I said, "I guess he is too busy visiting all the human children to have much time left for animals." "You see. Santa Claus is only for human children," Fritz said to Emily, "So, forget about the whole idea. Let's go home now before you catch a cold."

# 105. True Wealth (Baghdad)

Once upon a time, there lived a very rich and wealthy man in a big town. He always boasted his luxurious life to his friends and relatives. The rich man wanted to show off how rich he was. He planned for a day's visit to the entire town to show his son the life of poor people. They returned home after two days. The rich man asked his son, "Have you enjoyed it? So, what did you learn from the trip?" father asked, "Finally you have realized how the poor suffer and how they actually are." "No father," replied the son. He added, "We have only two dogs and they have 10 dogs. We have a big pool in our garden but they have a massive bay without any ends! We have a house in a small piece of land but they have abundant fields that go beyond the sight. We are protected by huge and strong walls, but they bond with one another and surround themselves. We buy foods from them but they are so rich to cultivate their own food." The rich father was stunned to hear his son's words and he was completely speechless.

# 106. Strong or Weak (Australia)

There was a proud teak tree in a forest. He was tall and strong. There was a small herb next to the teak tree. The teak tree said, "I am very handsome and strong. No one can defeat me." Hearing this the herb replied, "Dear friend, too much pride is harmful. Even the strong will fall one day." The teak ignored the herb's words. He continued to praise himself. A strong wind blew. The teak stood firmly. Even when it rained, the teak stood strong by spreading its leaves. At the same time, the herb bowed low. The teak made fun of the herb. One day, there was a storm in the forest. The herb bowed low. As usual, the teak did not want to bow. The storm kept growing stronger. The teak could no longer bear it. He felt his strength giving way and fell down. This was the end of the proud tree. When everything was calm, the herb stood straight. He looked around. He saw the proud teak had fallen. We should never underestimate others and make fun of them.

# 107. The Firefly (Japan)

A young man of Matsue was returning home from a wedding party when he saw, just in front of his house, a firefly. He paused for a moment and was surprised to see such an insect on a cold winter's night with snow on the ground. While he stood and meditated, the firefly flew towards him. The young man struck at it with his stick, but the insect flew away and entered the garden adjoining his own. Next day, he called at his neighbour's house and was about to relate the experience of the previous night when the eldest daughter of the family entered the room and exclaimed, "I had no idea you were here, and yet a moment ago you were in my mind. Last night, I dreamt that I became a firefly. It was all very real and very beautiful, and while I was darting hither and thither I saw you, and flew towards you, intending to tell you that I had learnt to fly, but you thrust me aside with your stick, and the incident still frightens me."

# 108. Babouscka (Russia)

It was the night when dear Child Christ came to Bethlehem. In a country far away from Christ, an old woman named Babouscka sat in her snug little house by warm fire. She heard a loud rap at her door. She opened it and her candle shone on three old men standing outside in the snow. "We have travelled far Babouscka," they said, "We stop to tell you of the Baby Prince born in Bethlehem. He comes to rule the world and teach all men to be loving and true. We carry His gifts. Come with us, Babouscka." "It is too late for me to go with you, good sirs," she said, "The weather is too cold." She went inside again and shut the door. The old men journeyed on to Bethlehem without her. So when it was morning, Babouscka put on her long cloak and took her stuff; she filled her basket with the pretty things a baby would like--and set out to find Child Christ. But none could tell her the way; she travelled for years but she never found the little Child Christ. They say that old Babouscka is travelling still, looking for Him.

# 109. Change Yourself and Not the World (India)

Long ago, people happily lived under the rule of a king. The people were very happy as they had a very prosperous life. The king decided to go on a travel to visit the places of historical importance and pilgrim centres. He decided to travel on foot to interact with his people. After several weeks, he returned to the palace. He had intolerable pain in his feet as it was his first trip on foot to a longer distance. He complained to his minister that the road was not comfortable and was very stony. He could not tolerate the pain as he walked all the way through the rough path. He ordered to make the road with leather. The ministers were disturbed with his order as they had to kill all cows. So they decided to make a piece for the king's feet. This is what we call now shoes.

# 110. The Sack (The Middle East)

Once upon a time in the Middle East, there lived a man named Mulla. He was always happy and gay. He wanted to see everyone happy. He used to help people in their bad times and participate in all activities. He himself was a wanderer. One day, Mulla came upon a frowning man walking along the road to town. "What's wrong?" he asked. The man held a tattered bag and moaned, "All that I own in this wide world is this miserable, wretched sack." "Too bad," said Mulla, and with that he snatched the bag from the man's hands and ran down the road with

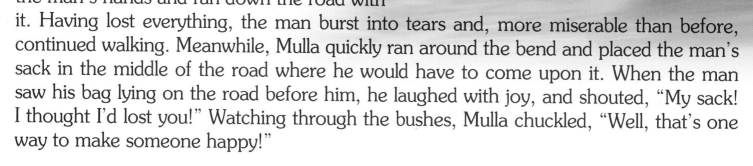

it. Having lost everything, the man burst into tears and, more miserable than before, continued walking. Meanwhile, Mulla quickly ran around the bend and placed the man's sack in the middle of the road where he would have to come upon it. When the man saw his bag lying on the road before him, he laughed with joy, and shouted, "My sack! I thought I'd lost you!" Watching through the bushes, Mulla chuckled, "Well, that's one way to make someone happy!"

# 111. The Purse of Gold (A Jewish Folktale)

A beggar found a leather purse that someone had dropped in the marketplace. Opening it, he discovered that it contained a 100 pieces of gold. Then he heard a merchant shout, "A reward! A reward to the one who finds my leather purse!" Being an honest man, the beggar came forward and handed the purse to the merchant saying, "Here is your purse. May I have the reward now?" "Reward?" scoffed the merchant, greedily counting his gold, "Why? The purse I dropped had 200 pieces of gold in it. You've already stolen more than the reward! Go away or I'll tell the police." "I'm an honest man," said the beggar defiantly, "Let us take this matter to the court." In the court the judge patiently listened to both sides of the story and said, "I believe you both. Justice is possible! Merchant, you stated that the purse you lost contained 200 pieces of gold. Well, that's a considerable cost. But the purse this beggar found had only a 100 pieces of gold. Therefore, it couldn't be the one you lost." And, with that, the judge gave the purse and all the gold to the beggar.

# 112. The Stolen Axe (China)

In China, there was a woodcutter who used to depend on woods for his living. One day, the woodcutter went out to cut some firewood and discovered that his favourite axe was missing. He couldn't find it anywhere. Then he noticed his neighbour's son standing near the woodshed. The woodcutter thought, 'Aha! That boy must have stolen my axe. I see how he lurks about the shed, shifting uneasily from foot to foot, greedy hands stuffed in his pockets, a guilty look on his face. I can't prove it, but he must have stolen my axe.' A few days later, the woodcutter was surprised and happy to come upon the axe under a pile of firewood. "I remember now," he said, "Just where I'd left it!" He felt very sad that he was thinking that the boy had taken his axe. The next time he saw his neighbour's son, the woodcutter looked intently at the boy, scrutinizing him from head to toe. 'How odd!' he thought, 'This boy has lost his guilty look. We always doubt wrong things when we are in trouble.'

# 113. The Gift for the Youngest Child (West Africa)

Once in a town of Africa, a great warrior did not return from the hunt. His family gave him up for dead, all except his youngest child who each day would ask, "Where is my father? Where is my father?" The child's elder brothers were magicians. The younger kid requested his elder brothers to find and bring his father home. Finally, the elder brothers went forth to find him. They came upon his broken spear and a pile of bones. The first son assembled the bones into a skeleton; the second son put flesh upon the bones; the third son breathed life into the flesh. The warrior arose and walked into the village where there was great celebration. He said, "I will give a fine gift to the one who has brought me back to life." Each one of his sons cried out, "Give it to me, for I have done the most." "I will give the gift to my youngest child," said the warrior, "For it is this child who saved my life. A man is never truly dead until he is forgotten!"

# 114. The Lion and the Rabbit (India)

There was a lion that used to kill all animals in a forest. The animals of the forest made a bargain with a ferocious lion that killed for pleasure. It was agreed that one animal each day would willingly come to the ferocious lion's den to be his supper and, in turn, the lion would never hunt again. The first to go to the lion's den was a timid rabbit, who went slowly. "Why are you late?" the lion roared when the rabbit arrived. "I'm late because of the other lion," said the rabbit. "In my jungle? Take me to the other lion." The rabbit led the lion to a deep well and told him to look in. The lion saw his own reflection in the water and roared! The sound of his roar bounced right back at him as an echo. "I alone am king of this jungle," he roared again. His echo answered him, "I alone am king of this jungle." With that, the lion became so enraged that he charged into the deep well with a great splash! The lion attacked his own reflection and was never heard again.

# 115. You Don't Know (Eastern Europe)

Once upon a time in a village, a pious old man would each day cross the village green and go into the temple to pray. A soldier watched him doing this day after day. One morning,

out of ill-temper, the soldier stopped the old man and said, "Where do you think you're going?" "I don't know," replied the old man. "What do you mean you don't know?" said the soldier, "Every day I see you walk out of your house at this time, cross the village and go into the temple to pray. Answer me! Where are you going?" Again, the old man replied, "I don't know." With that, the soldier grabbed him by the scruff of the neck, took him to the jail and pushed him into a cell. Just as the soldier was turning the key, the old man looked at the jail and said, "See! You don't know!" The soldier looked intently at the old man; he felt very sorry for his behaviour and took the old man to the temple. It was the first time the soldier was going inside the temple.

# 116. The Boatman (The Middle East)

One day, a scholar had to cross the river. He saw a boatman near the bank of the river. The scholar asked the boatman to row him across the river. The journey was long and slow. The scholar was bored, so he started his conversation with the boatman, "Boatman," he called out, "Let's have a conversation." Suggesting a topic of special interest to himself, he asked, "Have you ever studied phonetics or grammar?" "No," said the boatman, "I've no use for those tools." "Too bad," said the scholar, "You've wasted half your life. It's useful to know the rules." Later, as the rickety boat crashed into a rock in the middle of the river, the boatman turned to the scholar and said, "Pardon my humble mind that to you must seem dim, but, wise men, tell me, if you ever learnt to swim." "No," said the scholar, "I've never learnt. I've immersed myself in thinking." "In that case," said the boatman, "you've wasted all your life. Alas, the boat is sinking." The boatman hurriedly swam across the river and saved himself.

# 117. The Banquet (The Middle East)

One day, there was a banquet ceremony arranged by the king in the palace. A poor man dressed in rags came to the palace to attend the banquet. Out of courtesy he was admitted but, because of his tattered clothing, he was seated at the very end of the banquet table. By the time the platters arrived at his seat, there was no food left on them. So, he left the banquet, returning several hours later dressed in robes and jewels he had borrowed from a wealthy friend. This time he was brought immediately to the head of the table and, with great ceremony, food was brought to his seat first. "Oh, what delicious food I see being served upon my plate!" He rubbed one spoonful into his clothes for every one he ate. A nobleman beside him, grimacing at the mess, inquired, "Sir, why are you rubbing food into your fine clothes?" "Oh," he replied with a chuckle, "Pardon me if my robes now look the worst. But it was these clothes that brought me all this food. It's only fair that they should be fed first!"

# 118. Fate (A Hebrew Folktale)

One day, King Solomon's servant came breathlessly into the court, "Please, let me borrow your fastest horse!" he said to the King, "I must be in a town ten miles south of here by nightfall!" King was perplexed what the reason was. "Why?" asked King Solomon. "Because," said his shuddering servant, "I just met Death in the garden! Death looked at me in the face! I know for certain I'm to be taken and I don't want to be around when Death comes to claim me! I want to go away from Death." "Very well," said King Solomon, "My fastest horse has hooves like wings. Take him." Then Solomon walked into the garden. He saw Death sitting there with a perplexed look on its face. "What's wrong?" asked King Solomon. Death replied, "Tonight I'm supposed to claim the life of your servant whom I just saw in your garden. But I'm supposed to claim him in a town ten miles south of here! Unless he had a horse with hooves like wings, I don't see how he could get there by nightfall."

# 119. New Shoes (China)

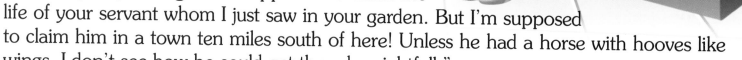

There lived a man in a small village in China. He was an eccentric man. His old shoes were worn out. So, he decided to buy a new pair of shoes. Before he went to the marketplace, he drew a detailed picture of his feet on a piece of paper, carefully measured them, and wrote down all their dimensions. Then, he set off on foot for the shoe store. Arriving

later that day at the marketplace, he unhappily discovered that he had forgotten to bring the paper with his measurements on it! He turned around and walked back home to get it. It was sunset by the time he returned again to the market, and all the shops were closed. He saw only one shopkeeper who was about to close his shop too. He explained his situation to the shopkeeper who had already packed away all his wares. "Foolish man!" said the shopkeeper, "You could have trusted your feet and tried the shoes on in the store! Why did you go home to get your diagrams?" The man blushed, "I guess I trusted my measurements more."

# 120. The Golden Touch (Greece)

Once there was a king named Midas who did a good deed for a Satyr and was granted a wish by the god of wine, Dionysus. For his wish, Midas asked that whatever he touched would turn to gold. Although Dionysus tried to dissuade him yet Midas insisted that the wish was an excellent one, and it was granted! Excitedly, Midas went about touching all sorts of things, turning them into gold. Soon Midas became hungry. He held a morsel of food in his hand, but couldn't eat it, for it had turned to gold in his hand! "I'll starve," moaned Midas, "Perhaps this was not such a good wish after all!" He thought and remained hungry. Midas' beloved daughter, seeing his dismay, threw her arms about him to comfort him, and, she too turned to gold! "The golden touch is no blessing," cried Midas. He went to the river and wept. The sand of that river turned as yellow as fool's gold for it was there, they say, that King Midas washed away the curse of the golden touch with his own tears.

# 121. The Skull (West Africa)

One day in a forest in Africa, a hunter came upon a huge tree with a whitened skull at its base. The skull spoke, "Beyond a certain hill is a field of calabashes. Take them to your hungry village, but do not tell anyone how you obtained them." "How did you come to be here?" asked the hunter. "My mouth killed me," said the skull. The hunter returned to the village with the calabashes but he could not keep the secret and immediately told everyone, "A talking skull showed me a field of food!" The Chief called him a liar. The hunter told, "Then come with me! I'll prove what I say is true." When they arrived at the tree, the hunter spoke to the skull but it remained silent. The villagers became very angry and they started beating the hunter; the hunter was put to death on the spot for lying. In time, two whitened skulls sat beneath the tree. The first turned to the second and said, "See; in death we meet again, my kin. It's true a mouth can do you in!"

# 122. The Fighting Rooster (A Taoist Tale)

Once upon a time in a village there was a man who had many hens and roosters. He wanted his fighting rooster to be more ferocious. So to train his rooster, he took the rooster to a trainer. In a few weeks' time he returned and saw that his rooster didn't squawk as loudly. "Not ready yet," said the trainer. A week passed. His rooster looked as tame and docile as a chick. He had no energy to walk and run and forgot about fighting. "You've ruined my fine fighting bird!" screamed the man at the trainer. He was so angry that he wanted to kill the trainer. "Not at all," the trainer replied, "See how calm and secure he is; how serenely strong he stands today. The other fighting birds take one look at him and they all run away." He had become a weak fellow who could die any time soon.

# 123. A Big Quiet House (Eastern Europe)

Once there was an old man who wished his small, noisy house would be larger and quieter. He went to a wise old woman of the town and explained his need. She said, "I can solve your problem. Just do as I say." The man agreed to do as she said. "If you have a chicken, a sheep, a horse and a cow," she said, "bring them into the house with you." 'That's a silly thing to do,' thought the old man. But he did it anyway. He brought the four animals inside his house. His house was already small, and with all those animals in it, there was no room at all. He got really frustrated. He returned to the old woman and cried, "I need more room! The animals are so noisy that I can't think!" "Take all those animals out of your dwelling," she replied. When he had put all the animals comfortably back in the barn, the man went into his house. To his amazement, it suddenly looked remarkably bigger! Without the animals inside, his house was now quiet too!

# 124. The Talkative Turtle (India)

There lived a talkative turtle in a forest. The turtle overheard two hunters say that they were planning to catch turtles the very next day. When the hunters left, the turtle asked two cranes to help him escape. "Beautiful white birds," he said, "if you hold a long stick between your beaks, I'll close my mouth tightly in the middle of it, and then you can fly up and carry me to safety." "Good idea," said the cranes. "But, for the plan to succeed, you will have to keep your mouth closed tightly on the stick and you must not say a word!" The turtle agreed and biting on the middle of a stick held in the beaks of two birds, off he was carried. When the birds were high in the air with the turtle dangling down from the stick, some people on the ground looked up at the strange sight in the sky and said, "What clever birds! They figured out how to carry a turtle!" The proud, talkative turtle cried out, "It was my idea!" and he fell tumbling down to earth.

# 125. Anansi Goes Fishing (West Africa)

Foolish Anansi thought he could trick a fisherman into doing his work for him. "Let's go fishing," he suggested. "Very well," said the fisherman, who was clever and quite wise to Anansi's tricks. "I'll make the nets and you can get tired for me." "Wait," said Anansi, "I'll make the nets and you can get tired for me!" Anansi made nets as his friend pretended to be tired. They caught four fishes. The fisherman said, "Anansi, you take these. I'll take tomorrow's catch. It might be bigger." Greedily imagining the next day's catch, Anansi said, "No, you take these and I'll take tomorrow's fish." But the next day, the nets were rotting away and no fish was caught. The fisherman said, "Anansi, take these rotten nets to the market. You can sell them for much money."

When Anansi shouted, "Rotten nets for sale!" in the marketplace, people beat him with sticks. Anansi said to the fisherman as he rubbed his bruises, "I took the beating. At least you could have taken the pain." Anansi never tried to trick the fisherman again!

# 126. Why Turtles Live in Water (West Africa)

It is said that Turtles used to live on land until the time a clever turtle was caught by some hunters. They brought him to their village and placed the turtle before the Chief, who said, "How shall we cook him?" They were wondering how to cook him when... "You'll have to kill me first," said the turtle, "and take me out of this shell." "We'll break your shell with sticks," they said. "That'll never work," said the turtle, "Why don't you throw me into the water and drown me?" "Excellent idea," said the Chief. Everyone agreed with the chief. They took the turtle to the river and threw him into the water to drown him. They were congratulating themselves on their success in drowning the turtle, when two little green eyes poked up in the water and the laughing turtle said, "Don't get those cooking pots out too fast, foolish people!" As he swam away, he said, "I think I'll spend most of my time from now on safely in the water." It has been that way ever since!

# 127. One Good Meal Deserves Another (West Africa)

Anansi, the Spider hated to share! When Turtle came to his house at mealtime, he said, "I can't give you food until you've washed your dusty feet!" Turtle licked his lips when he saw the big plate of steaming food, but politely walked to the stream to wash his feet. When he returned, the plate was empty. "Good meal," Anansi said, patting his full stomach. The turtle was going home hungry but before he left he offered Anansi to come and eat dinner at his place. "One good meal deserves another!" said Turtle, "Come to my house for dinner tomorrow." Turtle fixed a fine dinner at the bottom of the river. "Come down and eat!" he said. Anansi filled his jacket pockets with stones so that he might be weighed down enough to stay at the river's bottom and eat. "It's impolite to wear a jacket to dinner!" Turtle said, "Take it off!" But when greedy Anansi took off his jacket, he floated back up to the surface of the water and hungrily watched Turtle eat his fill! Turtle had taken his revenge.

# 128. Why the Sun and the Moon Live in the Sky (Africa)

Many years ago, the sun and the water were great friends. The sun asked water why he never visited him. The water then said, "If you want me to visit you, you will have to build a very large house." The sun began building a large house to entertain the water and all his people. When it was completed, the sun asked the water to come and visit him. When the water arrived, one of his people called out to the sun, and asked him whether it would be safe for the water to enter, the sun answered, "Yes, do come in." The water began to flow in, followed by the fish and all the other water animals. The water soon overflowed the top of the roof, and the sun and the moon were forced to go up into the sky...and they have been there ever since.

# 129. The Lucky Fisherman (Nigeria)

In the olden days, there were no hooks or casting nets. When the natives wanted to catch fish, they made baskets and set traps at the river side. One man named Akon Obo, who was very poor, made baskets. In the night a big fish used to smell the palm-nuts and go into the trap and in the morning Akon Obo would go and take the fish out. He was very successful in his fishing and used to sell the fish in the market for plenty of money. He married a woman named Eyong, a native of Okuni, and had three children by her. He still continued his fishing. The eldest son was called Odey, the second Yambi and the third Atuk. He gradually became wealthy and bought plenty of slaves. At last he joined the Egbo society and became one of the chiefs of the town. Even after he had become a chief, he and his sons still continued to fish. One day, when he was crossing the river in a small dug-out canoe, a tornado came very suddenly, and the canoe capsized, drowning the chief. They, therefore, called him the lucky fisherman.

# 130. The Striped Blanket (Philippines)

Once three Tinguian went to the mountains to hunt deer. They took their blankets with them, for they expected to be there for several days as nights in the mountains are cold. At night, the men rolled up in their blankets and lay down under a tree to sleep; but while the one in the striped blanket was still awake, two spirits came near and saw him. His blanket had red and yellow stripes like the back of a little wild pig. "Oh," he heard one spirit say to the other, "here we have something to eat, for here is a little wild pig." Then the man quickly took the blanket off one of his sleeping companions and put his own in its place. Very soon, the spirits came and ate the man under the striped blanket. Since that time the Tinguian never sleep under that kind of a blanket if they are where spirits can get them.

# 131. Wayambeh, the Turtle (Australia)

Oolah, the lizard, was out getting yams on a Mirrieh flat. She had three of her children with her. Wayambeh took her and her children to his camp. His tribe asked him if her tribe had given her to him. He said, "No, I have stolen her." "Well," they said, "her tribe will soon be after her; you must protect yourself. In a short time, the Oolah were seen coming across the plain which faced the camp of the Wayambeh. They were armed with fighting weapons. The chief said, "Now, Wayambeh, you had better go out onto the plain and do your own fighting; we shall not help you." Wayambeh chose the two biggest boreens that he had; one he slung on him, covering the front of his body, and one the back; he strode out to meet his enemies. Shower after shower of weapons they shot at him, and were getting at such close quarters that his only chance was to dive into the creek. He turned towards the creek and plunged in. Now a strange creature came out of the water which looked like him.

# 132. The Old Dog (Ukraine)

Once there was a man who had a dog. When the dog was young he was made much of, but when he grew old he was driven out of doors. "Look now," said the wolf, "I'm sorry for your condition; I will make things better for you. The mistress, I see, has put her child down beneath that wagon. I'll seize it, and make off with it. You run after me and take the child so that my mistress may see it." So, the wolf seized the child, and ran away with it, and the dog ran after him, and began to touzle him. His mistress saw it, and made after them with a harrow, crying at the same time, "Husband, Husband! The wolf has got the child! Gabriel, Gabriel! Don't you see? The wolf has got the child!" Then the man chased the wolf, and got back the child. "Brave old dog!" said he, "you are old and toothless, and yet you can give help in time of need, and will not let your master's child be stolen." And henceforth, the woman and her husband gave the old dog a large lump of bread every day.

# 133. The Blacksmith at Craig-y-don (Wales)

Once upon a time, an old blacksmith lived in an old forge at Craig-y-don. He used to drink a great deal of beer. One night he was coming home from an alehouse, very tipsy. As he got near a small stream, a lot of little men suddenly sprang up from the rocks and one of them came up to him and said, "If you don't alter your ways of living, you'll die soon; but if you behave better and become a better man, you'll find it will be to your benefit," and they all disappeared as quickly as they had come. The old blacksmith thought a good deal about what they had told him. He left off drinking, and became a sober steady man. One day, a few months after meeting the little people, a strange man brought a horse to be shod. Nobody knew either the horse or the man. The old blacksmith tied the horse to a hole in the lip of a cauldron that he had built in some masonry. The horse ran away with its master. When the old blacksmith came, he found three brass kettles full of money.

## 134. Spin-Spin-Spinning (Scotland)

Once, there was a gentleman who lived in a very grand house. He married a young lady. The man had everything but he wanted his wife to spin but she didn't know how to spin. One day, she saw six ladies singing and spinning in a cave. She said to them, "I do not know how to spin but my husband wants me to spin." The ladies told her to invite them to dinner when her husband came. They came and they all sat down to dinner. The husband, becoming familiar with them, said, "Ladies, why are your mouths turned away to one side?" "It's with our constant spin-spin-spinning," said the ladies. The gentleman cried, "I'll not have my wife to spoil her bonnie face with spin-spin-spinning." And so the lady lived happily with her husband all the rest of her life.

## 135. Lady Clare (Rome)

Lady Clare was in her garden overlooking the sea. Approaching Lady Clare, a knight saluted her and asked about her well being. The lady said, "Please marry one of my three daughters; I will give you gold and ivory." The knight said, "They are of no use to me as I am a warrior." "Do not call for thy vassals, for they are mine as well," said the knight, "and do not be angry with me, for I have already kissed you." "Then you are surely my brave lord," said Lady Clare, "but how will you prove yourself?" "By the golden ring with seven gems which I divided with you when I left," answered the knight, "Here is my half; where is yours?" "My daughters," cried Lady Clare.

# 136. The Islands of Flowers (Portugal)

Long, long, ago there was a little angel who broke one of the rules of Paradise. She was banished from her heavenly home. She filled her arms with the lovely blossoms of Paradise. Slowly and sorrowfully, she left the heavenly gardens. Some of them fell. Down, down to earth they floated. They came to rest on the smiling blue waters of the broad Atlantic. There were nine of the flowers of Paradise which the angel dropped. They have always remained in the blue Atlantic where she left them. After many years the Portuguese mariners found them and Portugal claimed them as her own. She named them the Azores. To this very day, however, one of the islands is called Flores, which means flowers.

# 137. The Forest of Lilacs (France)

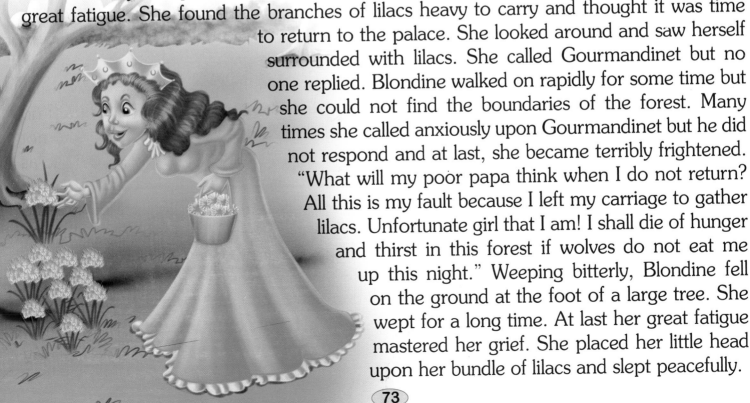

When Blondine entered the forest for gathering the beautiful branches of lilacs, she became busily occupied for about an hour. She began to suffer from the heat and to feel great fatigue. She found the branches of lilacs heavy to carry and thought it was time to return to the palace. She looked around and saw herself surrounded with lilacs. She called Gourmandinet but no one replied. Blondine walked on rapidly for some time but she could not find the boundaries of the forest. Many times she called anxiously upon Gourmandinet but he did not respond and at last, she became terribly frightened. "What will my poor papa think when I do not return? All this is my fault because I left my carriage to gather lilacs. Unfortunate girl that I am! I shall die of hunger and thirst in this forest if wolves do not eat me up this night." Weeping bitterly, Blondine fell on the ground at the foot of a large tree. She wept for a long time. At last her great fatigue mastered her grief. She placed her little head upon her bundle of lilacs and slept peacefully.

# 138. The Giant (Eskimo Folktale)

In the olden days, an enormous man lived with the other members of the Inuit tribe in a village. He was so tall that he could straddle the inlet, and ate the whole whale just as other men ate a small fish. One day, all the natives were having a hard time to hold and keep their boats from capsizing; he rose and strolled down to the shore and scooped the whale and the boats from the water and placed them on the beach. "You had better be careful," said the people, "for a couple of huge bears have been seen near the village." "Oh, I don't care for them. If they come too near me, throw some stones at me to wake me up," he said with a yawn. The bears came, and the people threw the stones and grabbed their spears. The giant woke up. "Where are they? I see no bears." he asked. "There! There! Don't you see them?" cried the Inuit. "What! Those little things! They are not worth this entire bustle." And he crushed one between his fingers and put the other into the eyelet of his boot to strangle it.

# 139. Beth Gellert (Celtic Folktale)

Prince Llewelyn had a favourite dog, greyhound named Gellert that had been given to him by his father-in-law, King John. He was as gentle as a lamb at home but a lion in the chase. One day, Llewelyn went to the chase and blew his horn in front of his castle to call Gellert but he did not come. He was angry and left for the forest with other dogs. When he returned, he saw Gellert greeting him with blood in his mouth. He became suspicious that Gellert used to play with his little son Prince Llewelyn. He went inside looking for his son. He could not find him. Out of rage he killed Gellert. But later, he found his son and a wolf killed by his dog Gellert. In vain was all Llewelyn's grief; he could not bring his faithful dog to life again. So, he buried him outside the castle walls within sight of the great mountain of Snowdon, where every passer-by might see his grave. He raised over it a great cairn of stones. And to this day, the place is called Beth Gellert or the Grave of Gellert.

# 140. Peter-of-the-Pigs (Portugal)

Long ago, there lived a man who employed a boy named Peter to take care of his pigs. One day, a man came up to Peter and said, "Sell me these seven pigs." Peter sold six pigs and buried the ears and tails of pigs in sand and called his master. His master ran. There, he saw one of the pigs halfway out of the sand. He and Peter together soon pulled it out completely. To his horror, he saw six tails coming. "Run to the house and ask my wife to give you two shovels!" cried the owner of the pigs, "With the shovels we can dig out the rest of the pigs." The boy ran to the house. He knew that his master kept his money in two big bags. So, he asked for the two bags. His wife gave him both the bags after confirming it with her husband. Thus Peter received his master's two bags of money. But a robber took all his money. When at last Peter's master found him, he was dead. He said, "Oh, Peter-of-the-pigs! You were sharp, but you found someone who was sharper."

# 141. The Princess of the Lost Island (Portugal)

Euphemia was the daughter of King Atlas and the grand-daughter of the great god Jupiter. She was more beautiful than her fifteen sisters, though they were all lovely. She decided to come down to earth. Now in the island of Seven Cities there lived a rich and venerable Christian prince. He adopted Euphemia as his own daughter. She was called Princess Euphemia of the island of Seven Cities. As soon as she came to the island, all pain and misery vanished from it. Euphemia herself remained always young, always beautiful. Two priests came to the city but they returned to tell everyone about this celestial place. Next morning, the island had entirely disappeared. The water stretched before their gaze with an unbroken rippling blue surface. "What has become of our beautiful island," the good priests asked in amazement. Euphemia, they say, has not yet disappeared entirely. She has changed her form. She is still found in the Azores in the plant called SOLANEA.

# 142. The Fox and the Hedgehog (Greece)

Once in autumn, a hedgehog and a fox ran into each other. The fox said to the hedgehog, "Come with me to the vineyard to steal some grapes." The hedgehog answered, "No, I am afraid of the traps they have set out there." The fox said, "Have no fear. You'll come to no harm, because I have three bags full of tricks." So, they went there together and ate until they were full, but just as they were leaving, the fox caught herself in an iron trap. She called out, "Help me, Hedgehog! I'm caught in a trap." He said, "Empty the tricks out of your bag, so I can free you." The fox said, "I jumped over a ditch and all my tricks fell out. Don't you know even one?" The hedgehog replied, "I know two of them. The one is that when the farmer comes, just play dead; the other is that while you are playing dead you should let a mighty fart." The fox did what the hedgehog had advised. When the farmer came by, he thought that the fox was already stinky rotten and he threw him out of the vineyard. Thus the fox escaped.

# 143. The Bear as Judge (Finland)

A dispute arose among a number of animals, namely the wolf, the fox, the cat and the hare. Unable to settle matters by themselves, they summoned the bear to act as judge. Everyone said, he had a hundred or thousand ways to escape. Only the cat said she had only one way to escape. Then the bear decided to put them all to the test in order to see how each one would save himself in time of danger. He suddenly threw himself at the wolf and crushed him half to death. Seeing what had happened to the wolf, the fox started to run away, but the bear grabbed him by the tip of his tail, and even to this day the fox

has a white spot on his tail. The hare, with his fast legs, escaped by running away. The cat climbed up a tree, and from his high perch sang down, "The one who knows a hundred ways was captured; the one who knows a thousand ways was injured; long legs must run on forever; and the one who has only one way to escape sits high in a tree and holds his own."

# 144. A Mantis Trying to Stop a Chariot (China)

When somebody over-rates himself, he is often warned: "Don't be a mantis trying to stop a chariot." The saying comes from a legend dated back to the spring and autumn period. One day, the King of Qi went out for hunting. The carriages were going along, when suddenly a mantis stood in the middle of the road.
It was obvious that he was trying to fight against the carriage to hold it back. Surprised at the case, the King of Qi ordered to stop and asked what creature it was. The King sighed with exclamation at its braveness. He mused a moment and added, "It's a great pity that it is not more than an insect. If it were a man, he must be the bravest warrior in the world!" Then the King ordered his carriages turn around it to leave the mantis there standing martially. When the persons around heard the King's words, they were well touched and determined to devote themselves to the country. As time passed, the meaning of the phrase changed to its opposite. Now it means that someone over-rates himself and tries to hold back an overwhelmingly superior force.

# 145. The Bear and the Travellers (Africa)

Two travellers were on a long journey through the countryside. They were walking along a track, they suddenly spotted a great bear ambling towards them. The first traveller climbed up the first tree and hid amongst the high branches. The second one dropped his bags and fell to the ground, pretending to be dead. He'd heard somewhere that bears don't like to eat dead flesh, so he thought this was his safest way to survive. The bear reached the spot where the man was lying on the ground. The man was keeping as still as he could, and doing his best to keep his breath in. The bear sniffed around his head for a few minutes, but did not seem to be all that interested, and went on his way. The second traveller gingerly climbed down from the tree to join his friend. "Phew!" he said, "That was close. From up there in the tree, I could have sworn that the bear was talking to you!" "He was," the second one replied, "He told me to be more careful in future while setting out on a journey, and not to travel with someone who deserts you at the first sign of trouble!"

# 146. Young Man Shows True Love (Malaysia)

Two hundred years ago, there was a princess named May Yee. She was born in Malaysia. She wanted to get married to a young man, but he was very poor. Her mother was very angry because she wanted to marry the poor young man. Her mother said, "Are you sure you want to get married to him? You know that you are the prettiest girl in the world." To that the princess said, "I know him. He is a good man. He loves me very much, and I love him too." One day, a fierce dragon appeared in their town. It killed a lot of the villagers. Then the Queen said whoever killed the dragon would get his wish granted by her. The young man said to the Queen that he would go. He said to the princess, "Don't worry about me. I will kill the dragon. After that we can get married." Then he went out to kill the dragon. The dragon was very strong and they fought a great battle. The young man killed the dragon, but not before the dragon injured him. The princess was so happy that she cried. After that the queen agreed to her daughter's wish. They got married, and they became a couple.

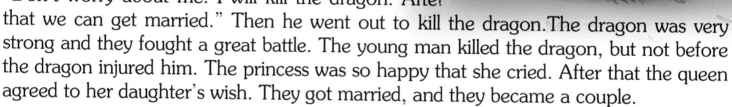

# 147. Brothers (Korea)

A long, long time ago, there lived two brothers in a village. They both were very poor. The elder brother had a little more than the other one. He had a larger family to support than the younger brother. One autumn, they harvested their grain, but the elder one was worried about his younger brother, so at night he took some grain and secretly put it in the place where his brother stored his grain. Next day, even though he had done this yet his own grain supply was not reduced. The next night, he did the same thing and again the next day. Still, his grain supply was not diminished. It stayed the same. He thought it was strange, so he hid in the field to see what happened. A few hours later, he saw a person approaching. He went out to see who it was. The stranger was his brother who was also worried about his elder brother. Each night he had been taking grain to his elder brother to help him! This was true brotherly love. After that they lived happily during the rest of their life.

# 148. A Passive and Tailless Dassie (Africa)

Long ago, the lion was the only animal with a tail. One day, he decided that each animal should have a tail like him. So, he got tails made for all the animals in his kingdom. When he found all the task done, all his subjects were summoned to his cave to their respective tails. The animals were exhilarated to have something very elegant, what only a king was possessed with. They made their all possible preparation to reach over there except Dassie, who was notoriously famous for his inert and passive temperaments. He did not attend the gathering. He told the monkey to bring his tail but the monkey, who had been given a long tail, was infatuated with the small furry tail of Dassie, so he did not return the tail. He attached it with his long tail. Dejected and despondent, Dassie could do nothing except regretting, but he was too lazy to pursue the monkey in order to get his tail back. That is why he remains tailless to this day.

# 149. Little One Inch (Japan)

Once, a couple of Japan, after spending many years without any child started musing that why God brought this catastrophe to them. They so intensely longed of children that even a little inch-sized child could dispense merriment in their life. And they were blessed with a little-sized son as they wished, he was named Issun Boshi, 'little one inch'. When he turned fifteen, he set for the capital city in search of his fortune with a very heavy heart. At the workplace he successfully influenced his masters, but left immense impact on his master's daughter. Once they both had a visit to a temple, where they were stopped by two gigantic giants. One of them swallowed Issun to trouble the girl. Issun had a needle in his waistcoat, which he used to stab in the giant's stomach to come out of it. The giant feeling of excruciating pain in his stomach led him to vomit Issun out of the stomach. And as the other giant looked down to see Issun, he broke his eyes with his needle. This way he set him and the girl free of them. In their haste they left behind a mallet which Issun Boshi and the girl--she had come back to help him--recognised as a magical object. This enigmatic power transformed him into a normal-sized man and thus they agreed to get married to start a beautiful life ahead.

# 150. Lake Toba (Indonesia)

In ancient times, there lived an orphan peasant boy named Syahdan in Sumatra Island. Syahdan had to do farming and fishing. One day, he was fishing a very beautiful fish. The colour was golden yellow. So holding, the fish turned into a beautiful princess. Because a human touched, it turned into a princess. Fascinated by her beauty, Syahdan asked the princess to become his wife. She agreed on the condition that the young man would not tell their origins to anyone. Syahdan then agreed to all terms. After a year, the couple was blessed with a son. The son had a bad habit, that is he never satiated. He ate all the food there. One day, the child was eating Syahdan all the food from his parents' plate as well. The young man was very annoyed; he said, "The basis of the offspring of fish!" That statement by itself unlocked the secrets of what he had promised to keep. Their promise had been breached. His wife and son disappeared mysteriously. And from the ground of their former footing many water springs came out. Water flowing from the springs started increasing till it became a vast lake. The lake is now called Lake Toba.

# 151. The Laird of Balmachie's Wife (Scotland)

In the olden times, when it was the fashion for gentlemen to wear swords, the Laird of Balmachie went one day to Dundee, leaving his wife at home ill in bed. He encountered fairies which carried his wife in bedclothes. They disappeared on seeing him. He placed her on the horse before him, and, arrived safely at home. He placed her under the care of an attentive friend. He went to his wife's bed, lifted the impostor from the bed and threw her on the fire, from which she bounced like a sky-rocket. His wife said that after sunset, the nurse left her for preparing a little candle. Elves came in at the window, thronging like bees from a hive. They filled the room, and having lifted her from the bed carried her through the window, after which she recollected nothing further, till she saw her husband standing over her on the Cur-hills, at the back of Carlungy. The hole in the roof, by which the female fairy made her escape, was mended. But it could never be kept in repair, as a tempest of wind happened always once a year, which uncovered that particular spot, without injuring any other part of the roof.